AN

OCEAN

IN

IOWA

BOOKS BY PETER HEDGES

NOVELS

What's Eating Gilbert Grape

An Ocean in Iowa

PLAYS

Imagining Brad

Baby Anger

Good As New

Oregon and Other Short Plays

PETER HEDGES

———

AN
OCEAN
IN
IOWA

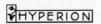

NEW YORK

DESIGNED BY DOROTHY S. BAKER

Library of Congress Cataloging-in-Publication Data

Hedges, Peter.

An ocean in Iowa : a novel / Peter Hedges. — 1st ed.

p.   cm.

ISBN 0-7868-6404-4

I. Title.

PS3558.E3165O28   1998

813'.54—dc21   97–40354

CIP

FIRST EDITION

10 9 8 7 6 5 4 3 2 1

For Marc H. Glick

CONTENTS

AN

OCEAN

IN

IOWA

WHAT SCOTTY SAID

When he was four or thereabouts, Scotty Ocean liked to stand on the piano bench while his mother, a painter of abstracts, played the only song she knew.

She practiced it daily, her eyes closed, a Salem cigarette burning in the nearby ashtray.

For Scotty there was no place better to be than at her side, where he might tug at her blouse or whisper in her ear or pound the black keys with his fists. But it hardly mattered what he did because when Joan Ocean played her song, everything— even Scotty—disappeared.

One day he said something that brought her to a stop.

She made him say it again. This time she watched closely as his pink lips shaped the sounds. She would never forget it. Later it would haunt her: his eyes, his voice, and the words, spoken simply . . .

"Seven is going to be my year."

ALMOST HEAVEN

(1)

In the summer of 1969, if you had asked the then six-year-old Scotty Ocean what a judge actually did, he couldn't have told you—and why his parents never hugged or kissed, he would have been at a loss—and why his sisters kept whispering, giggling about girl matters, he would've had no idea. Scotty Ocean was not in possession of all the facts.

But he knew some things. He knew where he came from. He knew his mother had made him. In her art studio. The same way she made paintings and sculptures.

"You made me, right?"

Joan always nodded a gentle yes.

"But just you."

Joan would try to include the Judge but Scotty would cover his ears and scrunch his face, insisting—"Only you made me."

Soon Joan stopped trying to tell him otherwise.

For Scotty, the particulars always changed. When his

mother experimented with sculpting marble, he was convinced that he, too, had been chiseled, and the unused parts of him had fallen to the floor like the slivers and chunks in the corner of Joan's studio. When she worked at her pottery wheel, he watched the way she would wet her fingers and stick a thumb in the spinning lump of clay—suddenly a shape. He would shout over the blaring radio, "This is how you made me."

Joan didn't bother to correct him. Scotty's beliefs were creative and she was the featured player in his wanderings—this charmed her, and why, she thought, why, as she popped open the next can of beer, why tell him the facts. He had his whole life to live with the facts.

(2)

The Judge had been standing at the top of the stairs, calling down to his wife for some time. "Joan," he said. "Come here."

Joan pretended she hadn't heard him.

"Honey," the Judge pleaded.

Joan called back, "We're in the middle of dishes."

Claire, their older daughter, helped clear the table while Maggie played on the kitchen floor.

"Honey, come here," the Judge begged. "It'll only take a minute."

Joan looked at her daughters both occupied and the dishes half washed. Then she turned and headed out of the kitchen. She went because in West Glen, Iowa, in 1961, when called, wives went.

"What is it?" Joan asked, climbing the stairs.

Judge Ocean did not answer.

"What do you want?" She looked for him in the bathroom. She walked into their bedroom. "Walter?" He was nowhere to be found. "This is no time for games." She sensed something behind her moving, so she turned in time to see the linen closet door swing open, only to find her husband standing in front of her, naked and erect.

She removed her apron and bent over their bed. While he moved above her, she thought about the flowers she would plant the coming spring.

When he finished, the Judge, gasping for breath, leaned over and stuck his tongue in her ear. "Don't," she said, and pulled up her underwear.

That night Joan sat on the living room sofa. In the kitchen, the Judge made popcorn using a pressure cooker. The sound of kernels popping had the girls jumping up and down. "Mommy," they shrieked. "What are we!"

Joan drew in on her cigarette and said nothing.

"We're popcorn!"

The girls slowed their dancing, then stopped. They studied their mother, who stared blankly at the turned-off TV, cigarette smoke leaking out her mouth.

Claire asked, "Mommy, what is it?"

"Nothing, honey."

But it was hardly nothing. She knew it; she felt it deep inside.

She had conceived.

When the Judge rounded the corner with his nightly bowl full, his girls leapt toward him, their little hands reaching up for the corn. With a girl on either side, he settled into the sofa. He lifted up the saltshaker. "Let me," the girls squealed. As each daughter took their turn, Joan Ocean started to cry.

. . .

Her first pregnancies had been remarkable experiences. In 1957, after reading the book *Childbirth Without Fear,* Joan informed her obstetrician, Dr. Charles Vernon, exactly how she intended her baby to be born. Dr. Vernon argued with her. He believed Joan was making a mistake. But in thirty years of delivering babies, he'd rarely met a woman so determined.

When it came time, Joan requested three pillows and refused to lie down and submit to the common medical practices of the day. With proper breathing and an unshakable belief that childbirth couldn't hurt too much, that for millions of years women had been giving birth, and that she was just another, a link in a long line, she gave birth to Claire the "natural" way in an eleven-hour period. Nurses who had been skeptical looked at her with a much deserved respect.

"Your wife is unusual," Dr. Vernon later told the Judge.

Maggie's birth proved even easier, done in eight and a half hours, and it confirmed Joan's thought that there was nothing nicer than giving birth.

But Scotty's labor would be different.

Joan, all sweaty and exhausted, shouted and moaned—endless contractions—she was to endure hours of pain.

"The little brat doesn't want to come out."

Dr. Vernon said, "You know, Joan, this doesn't have to hurt so much."

She shook her head, determined, her hands clenching the steel sides of her hospital bed.

"You know we can kill the pain. . . ."

"No!"

Joan held out. She had gone into labor on July 10, 1962,

and Scotty was delivered just after midnight on the twelfth. Twenty-nine hours—it was as if Scotty didn't want to be born.

Perhaps he knew he wasn't welcome, Joan told herself. Between contractions she vowed to work extra hard to like her child. Fortunately her guilt for wanting a miscarriage, her self-hate for wishing this baby had never existed, evaporated the first moment Scotty was set on her chest and went for her breast and missed.

"He'll learn," she told the Judge, who wiped her sweaty face with his handkerchief.

"Of course," he replied.

On the drive home from the hospital, the Judge remarked, "The doctor said you have an unbelievably high tolerance for pain."

The Judge turned onto their street.

"I thought you should know that's what he said. Very few people could take what you withstood. He was impressed."

Joan forced a smile for her husband. She knew he was proud of how she delivered.

The girls stood with Joan's parents on the porch. A sign hung on the garage door, painted in bright red and blue: WE'VE GOT A BROTHER. WELCOME HOME, SCOTT.

Later that afternoon, the Judge painted on a Y, explaining to the girls who watched, "Your grandfather, my father, was also named Scott. So we'll call your brother Scotty. Scott*eee*." Then the Judge went back inside, and the girls practiced saying their little brother's name.

Joan received visitors for most of that afternoon. Neighbors and friends stopped over. The Judge's secretary came with balloons. All guests were served pink lemonade and cookies compliments of Joan's parents.

While the Judge told the entire birth experience from his perspective (which consisted of his pacing the halls and napping in the waiting room), Joan sat at the kitchen table. The noise of children playing and the Judge talking in the living room blurred for her, and she looked down at her boy asleep in her arms, his crooked face, tiny eyes, his lips and nose so little.

In the living room, the consensus among the guests was that Scotty's looks favored his father, but the Judge was quick to disagree: "He doesn't look a thing like me. He looks like an hors d'oeuvre."

Hearing this, Joan thought the following, and pledged it to herself, as both prayer and promise: You will be loved, Scotty Ocean.

And while the guests laughed at the Judge's remark, Joan leaned over and softly whispered to her newborn son, "You will be loved."

(3)

On his last day as six, Scotty tagged along with his mother as she ran an afternoon of errands.

At Kmart, he stuck his hand in the back pocket of her blue jeans and gripped tight. They came to a stop at the party supply section and picked out paper plates, party hats, and noise-makers.

At the cash register, while his mom paid with a personal check, Scotty wandered off, and Joan was forced to look for him, checking Toys, Pets, and Sporting Goods. When she finally found him in Appliances, he was standing, mouth open in awe, staring at images of astronauts practicing weightlessness at their training facility. Sixteen television screens, different sizes with various hues and tints, but the same image—these were the astronauts of Apollo 11.

"Scotty?"

Scotty didn't answer. He imagined he was bouncing around in the aisles of Kmart, floating like the astronauts in their simulation tank.

"Scotty?"

He turned to his mother and waved in slow motion.

"Let's go," Joan said.

At Kenny Rayburn's, where Scotty got his hair cut monthly, Joan sat outside in front of the twirling candy stripe that spun forever upward. Inside, Kenny Rayburn used an electric razor to shave the back of Scotty's head. Using scissors he trimmed Scotty's bangs.

In the parking lot of Safeway, Scotty finished off a bottle of 7-UP and then asked for a sip of his mother's beer. They talked about Buzz Aldrin.

At Magill's Bakery, Scotty begged his mother to put the top down on her yellow convertible, and Joan couldn't deny him. She unlatched the car top. She nodded to Scotty, who pushed the button that started it all moving. The black top rose up, folded back into itself, and Scotty could see the sky, which was gray, bruised with rain clouds.

She told him to wait right there. He stood up inside the car. She watched as he flailed his arms and shook his head.

"You know what I'm doing?"

"No, I don't." A palsy, Joan wanted to say. Something spastic.

It was the beginnings of a dance.

"Seven," he said. "I'm seven."

"You're still six," Joan reminded him. Then she walked quickly to the store. The sound of thunder came from above. It would rain in minutes. Before going into the bakery, she turned to check on him. Scotty had continued his dance alone.

Joan gasped. Any guilt for not baking her own cake disappeared the minute she saw the detailed frosting design. She turned to the baker Jerry Magill and exclaimed, "It's wonderful!"

Using gray dye in the frosting, Jerry had created the surface of the moon. Frosting craters; a miniature lunar module built out of toothpicks; an astronaut figurine and seven candles with small American flags taped to the sides.

"It's a work of art," she said.

Jerry smiled. He'd been so pleased with the cake that earlier he'd photographed it for his scrapbook.

"It's a crime to eat it," Joan said. "This cake could be framed."

"That's quite a compliment coming from you."

Joan Ocean began painting the year Scotty was born, working in a rented studio behind a toy store and an Italian restaurant in Windsor Heights, an adjoining suburb. Her work had a small following, and Jerry Magill and his wife were two of her most loyal supporters.

"I want it to be a surprise," Joan said.

So Jerry Magill carefully set the moon cake in a box, taped it shut, then wrapped it in a white sack.

On the drive home, the cake box sat in Scotty's lap. He wanted to open it but he knew better than to ask. He had to wait.

Scotty put his hand on the stick shift so that when Joan needed to change gears, her hand would wrap around his and they would shift together.

In the distance, east of town, lightning flashed.

"Let's go down Buffalo Road!" Scotty shouted.

Buffalo Road was an unpaved back road that had as its highlight a bump. Whenever Joan sped over the bump at full speed, Scotty would lift off his seat several inches.

"Go fast, Mom."

"Not today."

"Pretty please," Scotty begged. He knew she was the only mother who would speed over the bump on Buffalo Road.

"Honey," Joan said, "I have to take it slow."

"No!" he demanded. "Take it fast!"

Joan simply pointed to the cake box resting on Scotty's lap, the cake box that covered up two thirds of her boy.

Lightning flashed closer and a rumble of thunder followed.

Scotty looked down. "Let's go slow," he said.

As Joan Ocean drove slowly, winding and curving as the road dictated, Scotty studied the cake box. He wanted to open it, to prove what he suspected to be true. But he needed no proof, for he knew from his mother's expression when she came outside, he knew from the triumphant manner in which she lit her cigarette, he knew that in his lap was the cake of his dreams.

"I don't remember," Maggie Ocean said, after biting into a corn muffin. "Uhm. Much about. Seven was the year I got to . . ."

"Maggie, chew before speaking," the Judge said.

"Okay, uhm . . ."

"Swallow."

They waited for Maggie.

At ten, her blond hair was shoulder length; her bangs were cut like Scotty's, a wedge across the forehead. She had a few large freckles. Tall for her age, skinny, narrow shoulders, she was all bone and eyes.

Finished swallowing, Maggie said, "Okay! Seven was good, I think? I think it was good?"

"Is it a question, Maggie?"

"No, Daddy, it was good."

The Judge turned to Claire, who wiped her mouth with a napkin before speaking. "Seven was a year of tremendous change. The Vietnam War accelerated, Martin Luther King gave the 'I have a dream' speech—"

Joan interrupted, "Honey, that was 1966."

"Yes, but Maggie was seven for much of 1966. I was speaking for Maggie."

"That's correct," the Judge said.

"I thought you meant you were seven . . ."

Claire smiled at her mother. "No, it would have been 1963 for me. Two weeks after Kennedy's assassination. How could I forget that?"

"I stand corrected," Joan said. "But let Maggie speak for Maggie, and you speak for yourself."

Without missing a beat, Claire said, "Seven was a great year for me. Boys weren't an issue, they were still smaller than the girls, and it was the year I began to read real books. So I remember liking seven."

Scotty stared at Claire, who at twelve looked like her mother. She wore her hair in the same style, straight, bangs behind the ears, and her mouth had the same thick lips.

"Uhm, you know what I think?" Maggie said. "I think . . ." She paused as she struggled for the right words.

Tired of waiting for Maggie to finish her thought, Scotty clinked his glass with his salad fork. His family turned to him as he shouted, "Me. Me, me, me!"

And it was then that the Scotty stories began.

The Judge told about a much younger Scotty trying to revive the dead rabbit. Claire remembered when on his fourth birthday Scotty tried to direct the traffic on Ashworth Road using a plastic police whistle. Joan recounted the time Scotty came home from kindergarten, packed a suitcase, and ran away. Later, when he was returned home, Joan opened the suitcase to find one side filled with his favorite toys. On the other side—and this was the detail that got them all to laughing— he'd packed only one thing: a large photograph of himself.

Their favorite Scotty story had taken place the previous February, when Scotty, a first grader, stepped outside during a sleet storm. His two sisters watched from the living room picture window. Bundled up in his winter jacket, a tasseled stocking cap, and his wool mittens, Scotty leaned over and licked the mailbox. His wet tongue fused with the cold metal. He could not move.

Claire and Maggie knew right away they hadn't thought it through, for they had dared him, and if he didn't get loose before their parents returned home, they would be blamed.

In moments the sisters were outside. Claire tried to uproot the mailbox. As she pulled at the wooden base, grunting and sputtering, she explained her thinking: "If we can get the box inside, his tongue will thaw." But even with Maggie helping, the mailbox was not to be moved. The previous summer the mailbox base had been set in concrete.

While the girls shouted frantically, Scotty struggled to be understood. "It's cold" is what he tried to say. But with his tongue stuck, it sounded like "ooosss koohhhd."

Joan and the Judge had gone to a Sunday brunch with friends. They would be home shortly, in good spirits probably, unless of course they saw their boy frozen to the mailbox.

So Claire and Maggie had no choice. They each grabbed a shoulder and hooked under an elbow and yanked suddenly without warning. Scotty brought his hands quickly to his mouth. All three stood quietly staring at the miniature pink circle of flesh still stuck on the mailbox.

"It looks like a little pizza," said Maggie without thinking.

As Scotty's eyes filled and his skin flushed bright red, he began to jump about in the slush. He fell on his knees in a remaining patch of snow.

Later, while wrapped in blankets, Scotty lay on the kitchen floor, his hand crammed in his mouth squeezing the tongue.

He breathed in short, quick spurts, and didn't move. A steady stream of tears ran down his face.

Claire checked the cabinet that contained medicines and Band-Aids. She removed a medicine bottle and said, "Mom uses this on cuts."

Maggie said, "Let's try it."

So they propped Scotty up.

Claire opened the medicine called tincture of Merthiolate. It came in a dropper. Its smell brought with it the memory of every bike crash and knee scrape. It would leave an orange stain but it would sterilize. And Claire thought it was important to sterilize.

But when she dropped the Merthiolate onto Scotty's outstretched tongue, he jerked back, stood up, and began to slap at his mouth. He ran around the house. His face turned purple and he finally dropped to the floor and thrashed about wildly.

As Maggie begged him to calm down—"PLEASE, PLEASE"—Claire knew she had no choice. She dialed the operator.

When the Judge turned his Dodge Dart at the bottom of the street, he was the first to see the flashing lights. Then Joan noticed and knew immediately who was hurt. "Scotty," she said.

Two paramedics were loading him into the ambulance as the Ocean car pulled into the driveway. Claire and Maggie began to cry the minute they saw the car. The girls tried to explain, they apologized, in desperation they lied and said it was Scotty's idea; Claire finished the explanation by recalling a

TV show where the kid didn't get stuck. Even TV was to blame.

The Judge told everyone to calm down. "The body knows how to heal," he said. "The body knows best and we've got to get out of its way."

Joan rode in the ambulance while the Judge stayed home. She kept her eyes on Scotty, who stared back at her. The ambulance worker had wrapped Scotty's tongue with gauze. Joan said sweetly, "This is one time you can stick it out and not get in trouble."

Later that day, after dressing in a parka and matching scarf, the Judge stepped outside. It was time for him to do his part. Since the incident, the weather hadn't cooperated. The sleet turned to a hard falling snow that had begun to blanket car windshields and sidewalks and the street. The Judge found the bad weather fitting. It felt Shakespearean, Greek.

Brushing away the accumulated snow with his gloved hand, the Judge stared at the mailbox, studying for a moment the sliver of Scotty's tongue. Then he prayed without kneeling (for his knees would get wet), but he prayed all the same: Please make this the deepest pain my boy will ever feel.

Back inside the house, the Judge boiled water. Using his gloves as potholders, he carried the pan out the front door and poured the hot water over the mailbox. Steam rose. He waited a moment and then using the pancake spatula, he scraped the mailbox clean.

The girls had gone to their rooms where they waited for news of their brother.

At the hospital, Scotty lay on a stretcher. As an overhead light blurred his eyesight, as a nurse with several tiny black hairs on her chin poked around in his mouth, as the intercom called for a certain doctor to go to a certain room and another doctor to go to another room, Scotty made a gesture that no one saw. He wanted his mother.

Joan had gone to the pay phone outside of the emergency room. Digging around the bottom of her purse, she found a nickel, put it in the coin slot, and dialed.

"Judge Ocean speaking."

Joan said, her voice shaky, "The doctors want to keep Scotty a little longer. It's more procedural than anything."

"Oh," the Judge said. It was silent on the other end. Neither of them knew what to say. Then the Judge spoke: "I disposed of the tongue."

There was another uncomfortable silence. Then Joan said, "Would you like to say something to Scotty?"

The Judge said, "No." He thought it was better for Scotty to rest. But before hanging up, the Judge said, "Tell him *Bonanza* is on tonight."

The Judge wrote the girls' orders down on a napkin and went to McDonald's. He didn't cook, and the girls loved McDonald's, and it would be his way to help begin the healing. For in the Ocean household, when one child hurt, everyone suffered in their own way.

It was during *Bonanza*, however, that the Judge felt a rush of regret. After all, Scotty's tongue had been torn up, not his ears—Scotty could hear. The Judge, angry at himself, wished he had said something to Scotty.

During a commercial he dialed the hospital and the operator put the call through to Scotty's room.

"Let me talk to Scotty."

"You can't," Joan said.

"Please let me talk to him."

"He's asleep now."

"Oh," the Judge said. "Damn." The Judge paused. "When Scotty wakes up, tell him *Bonanza* wasn't much this week. Tell him he didn't miss a thing."

After hanging up, the Judge hurried back to the television. It was the best *Bonanza* episode he could remember—the best one in years.

When word spread the following day at Clover Hills Elementary, a pack of boys—third and fourth graders mainly—made a pilgrimage after school. They sent Scotty's best friends, Dan Burkhett and Jimmy Lamson, ahead. The boys reported back that the mailbox had no tongue on it. This news noted, the gang of boys scattered and headed to their respective homes, disappointed.

Even though his doctor said he could resume talking immediately, Scotty said nothing for days. The only time he opened his mouth was to insert the straw used to drink his vitamin milk shakes. For the time being all his meals were to be liquid.

Scotty's first grade teacher, Mrs. Marilyn Sands, felt sorry for Scotty and only asked him yes or no questions. And even though he frequently gave the wrong answer, he was at least nodding and shaking—he was trying.

His classmates left him alone. They knew he had suffered in unthinkable ways, and that one day they, too, might lose a portion of their tongue on a mailbox.

That Wednesday, however, Mary Beth Swift came to school with her arm in a sling. She had broken her wrist the day before while roller-skating. Sympathies quickly switched to Mary Beth, who offered her classmates a choice of different-colored markers with which to sign her plaster cast.

On Thursday morning when Joan woke Scotty, he made a face like he didn't feel well. "Then you'd better stay home," she said.

She worked for his trust. Gaining it, she thought, he would confide in her—he would eventually speak. So she took him on secret trips. They drove all over West Glen and Windsor Heights playing the car radio loud. They drove to the liquor store and bought extra six-packs of beer. She hid them in the basement in suitcases.

That Thursday night Scotty sat silently at dinner, slurping at his liquid diet. The girls hated the constant attention he was receiving. Any kindness showed Scotty felt like a slap at them, punishment for daring him to lick the mailbox, punishment for being beautiful and smart and clever and popular. As the girls battled for attention, they began talking faster at dinner, fabricating stories. The meal became chaos.

The Judge said dinner was over and that the next night there would be a constructive discussion about the future. He asked his children to think about what they wanted to be when they grew up. He excused the girls, who began to clear the table.

That Friday, Scotty went with his mother to her studio. He watched her squeeze out the oil paints. He liked watching her mix colors, the big thick globs of paint stirred into every color imaginable. Joan set him up with a miniature easel and several containers of finger paints. When she finished a painting, Scotty hurried to finish one, too. They hung their work side by side. She explained why his paintings were brilliant. "The color," she would say. "The feeling underneath."

That afternoon, while Joan talked on the phone, Scotty put his nose up to her palette of oil paints and inhaled deeply. He loved the smell so he breathed in several times fast. He grew dizzy. He danced a bit. He thought sentences but said nothing. This was the closest he'd come to saying words.

At dinner the Judge asked his children the question "What do you want to be when you grow up?" Maggie said a model. Claire had many goals, numerous interests. Joan said it would take three lifetimes to do all that Claire wanted.

Then the Judge spoke again: "And you know what?"

"What?" Claire and Maggie said.

"You," he said, fighting a smile, "Can. Be. Anything." He smiled, shouted, "ANYTHING!" and then turned to Scotty.

"Young man, what do you want to be when you grow up?"

Scotty didn't answer.

The Judge told him to answer.

Scotty didn't move.

"Don't be shy. Tell me what you want to be."

He put his arm around Scotty and pulled him close. Joan started to object. The Judge said, "Shhhh."

Scotty squirmed in an effort to get away. But the Judge was strong. There was no escape. The more Scotty tried to wiggle free, the more his sisters laughed.

"You can be anything you want to be," the Judge said. "Imagine that. You can be anything."

"Yeah," the girls said.

The Judge said, "You just have to be something."

Scotty began to hold his breath.

Joan whispered, "Walter."

The Judge waved his hand for her to be quiet. "You don't want to grow up, Scotty, is that it? You don't have dreams?"

Scotty had begun to turn blue.

Sensing that this was nowhere near working, the Judge patted Scotty on the top of the head, grinned for the family, excused the girls to start clearing the table, and sent Scotty to his room.

Everyone did as the Judge said, except for Scotty, who sat motionless.

"You don't have to talk," the Judge said, annoyed. "But you have to go to your room."

Scotty began to move his mouth. No one could hear him, not even the Judge, who was spooning the last of the mashed potatoes onto his plate.

"Look," Maggie said. "Scotty's trying to talk."

Scotty's mouth moved more.

Joan leaned over and listened. Scotty's voice was a whisper.

Joan said, "Something about heaven?"

Scotty shook his head.

The Judge interrupted, "Heaven comes after you die. What do you want to do before that?"

"No," Scotty said just loud enough for everyone to hear. "*Seven*. I want to be *seven*."

(6)

Even now, after six months, they loved to retell the story. Claire did an imitation of Scotty announcing "I want to be seven!" which caught Maggie off guard. A stream of orange Hi-C shot out Maggie's nose and everyone started laughing. The Judge almost fell out of his chair. Joan wiped at her eyes and begged, "Stop, please."

When everyone caught their breath, the Judge raised his glass and said, "So, Scotty, tomorrow you finally get what you want."

Scotty smiled, revealing his uneven teeth.

"Let's drink to that, what do you say?"

They all lifted their glasses—clink.

That night Joan used a remaining shard of soap to lather her hands.

"Let it go, Mom," Scotty said.

She let the soap drop. Scotty searched the bottom of the tub. Finding it near the drain, he raised his arms into the air, holding the soap sliver like a trophy.

"Wash me," he said.

With her hands appropriately lathered, Joan began to soap Scotty's back.

"Starting tomorrow, Mom, I won't need this anymore."

"No?"

"No," Scotty said, "I'll do it by myself."

"Oh, you will, will you?"

"You'll see. I'll do most things by myself."

She soaped his pale arms and chest. Using her fingernails, she scratched lightly over his shoulders, and she considered that one day these boy-shoulders would be broad. Soon his sweet face would grow hair, his voice would drop, and his hands would get rough and callused. How, she thought, how do I keep you, Scotty, just the way you are?

But there was one habit of Scotty's that Joan wanted to stop. In the middle of most nights, he found his way to his parents' bed and climbed in between them. The Judge had discussed putting a lock on the door. But Joan felt there must be a gentler way.

So that night she asked him as she tucked him in, "Do you know the history of this bed?"

Scotty shook his head.

"When I was your age, it was mine."

"You weren't my age."

"Yes, of course I was." She combed back his wet bangs with her fingers and smiled. "And this was my bed."

"But now it's mine."

"No, it's my bed, Scotty. I'm loaning it to you."

Scotty said nothing.

How could she tell him that he wasn't wanted anymore in their bed?

She kissed his lips, click went the light, and with her hand on the doorknob, and moments before all would be dark, she said, "Scotty?"

"Yes, Mom?"

"Will you do me a favor?"

He nodded, for he would do any favor, anything, for her.

"You will?"

"I'll do you a favor," he said.

"Will you take care of this bed."

"Yes."

Joan said, "Will you keep it warm for me?"

LOOK AT SCOTTY GROW

West Glen, Iowa (population 15,991), was one of a cluster of suburbs located west of Des Moines.

In those days you still could drive a few miles out and be in farm country. Drive east on Interstate 235, and in minutes you'd be in downtown Des Moines with full view of the twelve-story Equitable Building, the KRNT Theater, and the State Capitol, a gold-domed building that shined on a sunny day.

West Glen boasted one of the finest school districts in the state. With only half of its land developed, the Judge knew, and Joan didn't argue, that West Glen was a town with a future. It could only grow.

The Ocean house was built in 1962 along with forty or fifty others in a five-block radius. It had all that a family could need. Over half an acre of land, four bedrooms, a modern kitchen with a state-of-the-art stove, refrigerator, and dishwasher. It was typical for the neighborhood. The Judge wanted something that didn't stand out. He had found such a house.

They bought it before construction had been completed, a month after Walter was made a judge by the governor of Iowa. Thirty-seven years old at the time, he became the youngest judge in Polk County. A new, larger house was needed, as Joan was about to give birth to Scotty.

With fake shutters painted light blue, a red brick first story, and a white wooden second story, the house had a slightly patriotic flair.

Upstairs, Maggie and Claire had rooms of identical size that faced each other at the end of the hall. Scotty's room, the smallest, looked out over the backyard and the younger of two willow trees. His room was closest to his parents' bedroom, which was at the top of the stairs, across from the bathroom.

Downstairs, a living room/family room boasted a new television with rabbit ears, a wooden coffee table, a long sofa propped up by books on one end, and a baby grand piano, where Claire and Maggie practiced for their weekly lessons.

The day they moved in, Joan had her daughters stand with their backs to the kitchen closet door. Resting a book on their heads, she drew lines that recorded their height. When Scotty could stand, she included him. Throughout the years, the marks climbed the door, becoming, as the Judge liked to say, "evidence that big things are happening."

The living room had a large picture window, which Joan decided was perfect for displaying the artwork of her children. During those first years, watercolor paintings and crayon drawings were taped in the window for all the neighbors to see.

One summer Claire made a snow scene out of construction paper, gluing tiny paper flakes to the page, coloring in a snowman and two girls pulling a boy on a sled. Joan hung Claire's creation in the window even though it was only June.

"Mom," Claire protested, "don't put it up now."

"Why not?"

"Because it's summer."

"People need to be reminded of winter. Winter is coming."

"Mom!"

"There's nothing worse than art that no one sees."

While Joan was out running errands, an embarrassed Claire took the snow scene down and hid it under the basement stairs. But Joan hunted it down and returned it to its rightful spot. Claire considered tearing it to pieces, but decided against it when she realized Joan would painstakingly tape it back together. The snow scene remained displayed in the window.

While other children filled in their coloring books, getting praise for staying in between the lines, the Ocean kids could be found painting their driveway, no lines or requirements. "Just paint!" Joan would shout. She'd supply them with water-soluble paints or colored pieces of chalk and turn them loose. On most days, primitive images, oftentimes resembling cave drawings, covered their driveway. They might trace each other, kiddie crime scenes with a rainbow of colors. On an average summer day all three Ocean children would be busy creating.

But the day of Scotty's party was not your average day.

The driveway had been rinsed clean the day before in anticipation of the party guests. A painted sheet hung across the garage door: SCOTTY = 7. A second banner covered the picture window with HAPPY BIRTHDAY, SCOTTY followed by three exclamation points. A cluster of multicolored balloons had been tied to the infamous mailbox, indicating that if you were looking for a party, you had come to the right place.

The invited guests included Scotty's best friends of the moment—David Bumgartner and Dan Burkhett. Other about-to-be second graders, Craig Hunt, Richard Hibbs, and Jimmy Lamson, came, too. Even Tom Conway from down the street was invited, at Joan's insistence, because Tom, Scotty's least favorite friend of the moment, was a neighbor, and he would see the other kids arriving, Joan said, and it would hurt his feelings. "And we don't want to hurt Tom's feelings, do we?"

Yes, we do, Scotty thought.

"There is nothing worse," Joan said, "than deliberate cruelty."

So when he opened the front door and found Tom Conway's chubby face and crooked smile staring at him through the screen, Scotty tried to be nice.

Tom held up a large square gift-wrapped box. "Happy birthday," he mumbled. Tom's gift was wrapped in the peach-colored sports page section of the *Des Moines Sunday Register*. The box was surprisingly light.

Scotty shook it but he heard nothing.

"Invite him in," Joan whispered to Scotty, who reluctantly ushered his neighbor inside.

In the kitchen Claire was mixing a pitcher of grape Kool-Aid. She whispered, "Of course, *he* would be first." Claire often seemed to articulate Scotty's feelings before he even knew he felt them.

Scotty said, "Yeah," and extending a paper cup, he waited for Claire to pour.

"And what do you bet, Scotty, he'll be the last one here."

"Yeah," said Scotty, looking out the window to the backyard where Tom Conway had gone and sat waiting for the party to begin. Maggie gave him a party hat, but the rubber band broke when he tried to stretch it over his chin.

Before long the others arrived. Dan Burkhett rode his Schwinn Sting-Ray. He kept telling Scotty how his birthday would be next. "I'm on deck," he said, "but even better, I'm gonna be eight." Scotty wished Dan would be quiet. But Dan kept telling anyone who would listen, "On September twenty-ninth, I'll be *eight*."

Later he was to say, "At my party we're going to have an actual Mexican piñata . . ."

Claire told Scotty to ignore Dan Burkhett. "Maybe he won't see eight. Maybe he'll get squashed by a school bus or drown at Holiday Pool. He *assumes* he'll turn eight. He doesn't know for a fact, does he?"

"Yeah," Scotty said.

Claire poured Scotty more Kool-Aid.

"Yeah," he said again, a Kool-Aid mustache having formed on his top lip.

In full swing, Scotty's party proved to be exceptional. The Judge turned on the sprinkler out back. The boys ran from side to side, leaping over the spraying water, giggling as their swimsuits were drenched. Claire supervised other party games—a game of horseshoes and kickball with old record jackets serving as bases. Later, she led the cleanup of plates and plastic silverware. Maggie took over the Kool-Aid detail and stirred packages of black cherry and lemon-lime into large glass pitchers. Whenever thirsty, the boys ran to the picnic table to get refreshed.

"A great party," the Judge said as he entered the house. "Where's your mom?"

Scotty shrugged even though he knew.

The Judge must have known, too, for he opened the basement door and called down.

"Honey, get up here. It's time to open presents."

David Bumgartner gave a talking G.I. Joe dressed in an astronaut outfit. With a head of fuzzy red hair and a bristled beard, this G.I. Joe said eight commands at the pull of the miniature dog tag. "Entering lunar orbit" was Scotty's favorite. Craig Hunt gave a Slinky; Richard Hibbs, a deck of cards; Dan Burkhett, a Matchbox collectors case. "The case stands up," Dan said proudly, "and it can carry seventy-two cars." Jimmy Lamson gave Scotty a Peanuts pennant. Scotty held it for all to see. It was bright yellow with Charlie Brown standing alone, the jagged line across his shirt and his one hair in place. In capital letters the following was written: I NEED ALL THE FRIENDS I CAN GET!

The gift from his family came with a card written in his mother's hand with the following inscription: "To Scotty, for studying the tiniest movements of life." Scotty ripped open the package. It was a Power microscope lab set. The box claimed that inside, twelve slides were already prepared for viewing. The lab came with test tubes and a dropper and a three-wing metal cabinet. Scotty said, "Wow." The other kids looked on, jealous. Except for Dan Burkhett, who said, "I got one that's better."

"But you didn't open mine," Tom Conway kept saying.

Tom had given Scotty the Time Bomb, a black plastic imitation bomb with a red fuse. As the party guests stood in an enthusiastic circle, the Judge twisted the bright red "fuse," winding it—the bomb began to tick. "Pass it," the Judge ordered. "But don't throw it." As the Time Bomb moved about the circle, faces got tenser; hands moved the Time Bomb along quickly, as if it were on fire.

When it went *bang* the first time, David Bumgartner had it in his hands. He fell over onto the grass. Richard Hibbs was next and he dropped into a sitting position. All the best people in the whole world are here, Scotty thought, and they're all getting blown up.

Only Jimmy Lamson and Tom Conway were left with Scotty in the circle when the bomb went off in Scotty's hands. He tucked it close to his stomach, broke from the circle, and in the middle of the yard, he did his best imitation of an actual explosion. He threw the Time Bomb in the air, while adding his own spit-filled sound effects—his arms stretched in opposite directions, he landed in the grass on his stomach with his legs splayed. "Blown to bits," he announced to his friends as he pushed up on his arms. "Mom!" he called out—he saw she was watching from the back porch. *"I was blown to bits."*

Joan smiled.

Scotty made a face at her as if to say, No dummy—you don't understand. "I'm gone, Mom. I'm in little pieces all over the yard."

Joan smiled and said, "That's too bad. I guess you'll miss the cake."

As the other boys ran toward the Ocean house, Scotty walked confidently, because he knew there would be no cake until he blew out the candles.

Tom Conway picked up the Time Bomb and followed after Scotty, saying, "Better be careful. Otherwise you'll break it."

. . .

From the kitchen the Judge called out, "Scotty, never seen a cake like this!"

The curtains had been drawn. Joan flipped off the lights and from the kitchen a comet of cake and flames moved toward the dining room where Scotty and his friends sat waiting.

Everything about the moon-landing cake was unique. It seemed larger than the usual birthday offering (it wasn't). Lit only by candles, the cake's craters of frosting appeared even more lifelike. One could imagine it already becoming a kind of benchmark—the cake to which all other cakes would be compared.

The Judge led the singing. Joan snapped a picture of Scotty staring at it, stunned, his hands holding his head.

The wax from the seven candles had begun to drip on the frosting.

"You better hurry," Maggie said.

Joan said, "Make a wish."

Scotty thought for a moment.

"Hurry," the party guests urged.

Joan took a second picture as Scotty blew with all his might, his cheeks puffed, putting out the candles.

Dan Burkhett asked Scotty what he wished for.

"If you tell, it won't come true," Tom Conway said.

Scotty pressed his lips together and said nothing.

When Scotty saw the Judge lift the knife, he shouted, "No!"

The Judge stopped.

"Don't! Don't cut it."

The Judge smiled. "There are traditions, Scotty, boys—at birthday parties you eat the cake. It's what people do."

And with that, he brought the knife to the frosting a second time.

Scotty screamed, "No! Leave it alone!"

No one wanted to eat the moon.

And when Joan tried to say as much, the Judge glanced at her, rage in his eyes, a smile pasted on his face.

Joan turned away.

Holding the cake knife, the Judge said, "Cakes are meant to be eaten." Then he methodically cut equal pieces. Once the first piece was put on a plate, it became more cake than moon, and Scotty forgot his objections. He took the cake in his hands. A shaken Joan readied the camera and there was a bright flash when Scotty took the first bite.

(2)

He'd been seven for two days and everything had been perfect.

"And now this," Scotty said, sitting Indian-style in front of the television.

"Yes," Joan said, watching from the sofa. "And now this."

The Judge had gone upstairs to wake the girls.

Scotty touched the screen and said, "They're already in there." Smoke billowed out of the rocket. "It's about to blast off—"

"Scotty," Joan said, "those numbers on the TV tell us how long it'll be. We've still got thirty-two minutes."

"Oh."

"Time for another bowl of cereal if you want."

With his eyes fixed on the television screen, Scotty lifted the empty bowl above his head. Joan knew the signal. She took the bowl, went to the kitchen where she poured him more cereal and milk, and put the bowl back in his hands, which had stayed in the air waiting.

The Judge came downstairs and said with a shrug, "Claire's in the shower. And Maggie won't wake up. They don't seem excited."

"Scotty's excited," Joan said as she disappeared into the kitchen.

On the television screen, Spiro Agnew sat with other dignitaries on a special platform.

The Judge sat on the sofa, pointed to the TV, and said, "There's our Vice President."

"Call if something happens," the Judge said. He stood and went into the kitchen.

Soon Scotty heard the sharp tones of his father's voice, the slamming of a cupboard, and he knew it was an argument. He could only hear the Judge's side because Joan always whispered when she was upset.

Scotty decided to keep his parents posted. "Twenty-seven minutes," he shouted. "Twenty-four minutes!" He forgot about what was on TV; only the clock in the corner of the screen held his attention. "Stop fighting," he wanted to shout, but he only managed to give his updates. "Twenty minutes!"

At seventeen minutes and counting, the Judge emerged from the kitchen and smiled his fake smile. He touched Scotty on the top of his head and said, "You're the man in the family while I'm at work. Okay, Scotty?"

"Okay."

The Judge smiled. He walked to the doorway. Standing at the bottom of the stairs, he shouted, "Girls! You don't want to miss history!"

After the Judge left the house, Joan emerged from the

kitchen. She lit a cigarette the moment the Judge's car started. She smoked three in a row. Before she went back into the kitchen, she told Scotty to call her when it got close.

"Sure, Mom."

He watched her walk away.

As the blast-off got closer, Scotty felt a sudden distrust for the clock. What if Neil Armstrong or Edwin "Buzz" Aldrin hit the wrong lever and the rocket accidentally took off? It could happen. He'd made this argument the previous day with Tom Conway, whose father was fighting in Vietnam. Tom said, "Mistakes don't happen in outer space." Scotty disagreed and threw a stick at him, cutting Tom's forehead. Tom ran home to tell his mother, who called Joan who spanked Scotty and then kissed him.

When Claire, her hair wet from the shower, and Maggie, still in pajamas, thumped down the stairs, Scotty called out, "Mom, it's close."

His sisters plopped down on the sofa. Maggie yawned. Claire cracked her back.

"Mom, it's thirty seconds!"

Claire told Scotty to move as he was blocking the TV.

"Mom," Scotty shouted. "It's almost countdown."

At "ten . . . nine," he screamed for her.

At "six . . . five," Joan came in the living room from the kitchen and saw Scotty holding his breath.

"Three . . . two . . . one."

"Sweetie, breathe."

The camera tracked the rocket. It started slowly—smoke and flames—it shot straight up, then it began to veer to the right. As it went higher, it got smaller.

Scotty shook his head. He couldn't imagine how they'd get back to earth. "How will they get back?"

"Getting out of the atmosphere. That's the tough part," Claire said. "Once you're out, you don't need much fuel."

"That's right," Joan said. "It's the getting away."

"Yeah," said Scotty.

Maggie smirked at Scotty. "What do *you* know," she said.

Later, after his sisters bicycled to Holiday Pool to swim, Scotty stayed fixed to the television. He wouldn't relax until the Apollo 11 splashed down, until Neil and Michael and especially Buzz Aldrin were back on earth, safe and sound.

During an interview with a scientist, Scotty broke away from the TV and headed toward the kitchen. There he saw his mother slouched in a chair, smoking and staring down.

He moved to the center of the room. His hands contracted into fists. He threw one hand up as the other came down all the while bobbing his head and shaking his left leg, his right, his left, his right.

"The seven dance," he said.

Joan Ocean tried to smile, but couldn't.

So Scotty knelt before her, wrapped his arms around her extended legs, and began kissing her white tennis sneakers while she smoked and cried. "Kissing machine," Scotty said. With his lips, he moved to her ankles, to her knees where he sucked a kneecap—he moved up her thighs. Using her free hand, she pushed on his head to keep him from going any higher. He smooched the air, making his exaggerated version of the kiss sound. But he pressed against her hand; he was strong and determined, and Joan was tired. She gave way and his lips shot for her stomach. When he tried to lift her flowered shirt, she stubbed out her cigarette in the ashtray and shouted, "No! Scotty, no!"

He froze. The tone in her voice did not sound like his mother. He looked up at her. She didn't smile. So he turned, ran out of the room, and waited at the top of the stairs for her to come after him. When she didn't, he ran to his closet and hid. It'll take hours for her to find me, he decided, and when she does, she'll say she's sorry. She'll feel bad. Then we'll go downstairs and watch TV, or maybe go for a ride to the Lil' Red Barn for gum and candy bars, or maybe she'll take me to the top of Buffalo Road and we'll speed down the hill with the top down.

Scotty crouched in his closet.

So much time passed that Scotty could see it: His hair turned gray, spots formed on his hands, wrinkles cut across his face, and his ears grew big and hairy. I'll be a skeleton, he thought, if she doesn't come soon. He stared at his hands, squeezed his eyes open and shut, blinking away the age.

With no sign that his mother would come for him, Scotty snuck back to the top of the stairs. He could hear Joan talking, but he didn't hear anyone talking back. Scotty moved down a step at a time until he was at the base of the stairs. He tiptoed down the hall. He peeked around the corner and saw her standing at the kitchen sink, the phone cord stretched to its limit, her back toward him. She spoke softly. She sounded upset. He knew what to do. Quietly opening the basement door, he snuck down the darkened stairs. Light poured in from two small basement windows. He made his way to the far corner of the back room where a second refrigerator stood, humming, almost purring. He pulled at the handle and the light from inside forced him to squint. The cool air washed over his face. He closed his eyes and with his hands located a can and pulled it from its plastic holder.

He moved fast across the basement floor, bumping into two barstools and a stack of old encyclopedias. She heard me, he thought. But he crept up the stairs slowly, just in case.

At the top, he cracked the door and saw that his mother had wrapped herself in the phone cord. He watched as she listened, her face in pain. "But," she said. "What do I do? My paintings don't make money."

She was talking to Liz Conway, he decided. Because this was how she always talked to Liz Conway.

She unwound herself from the cord with the phone away from her ear. When she freed herself, she put the receiver to her mouth and said a chilly "Easy for you to say."

After hanging up, she breathed out a heavy sigh and sat at the kitchen table. Scotty slowly pushed open the basement door. She didn't hear him. He moved behind her, inches from her head. He lifted the beer can to the heavens, pulled back the tab—it made a *click* sound—then the whoosh of compressed air releasing—Joan snapped her head in his direction. This she'd heard. Her eyes brimmed with tears, and a smile formed, the look of relief, and she said, "Little love, you just read my mind."

(3)

Joan's studio was a small apartmentlike space on University Avenue in the neighboring town of Windsor Heights. Located behind a row of stores (Anjo's Restaurant, Wirtz's Rexall drugstore, Doug's Toy World, and a State Farm Insurance office), it was ideal for her purposes.

"It's my place to escape," she liked to say.

Whenever Joan had painting to do, she'd leave Scotty, and sometimes Maggie, to play at their neighbors', the Conways.

Liz Conway was the red-haired mother of Tom Conway. They lived with Tom's red-haired sister in a split-level house across the street and three lots down. The Conways moved into the neighborhood in 1967, about the time their father, Sergeant Conway, had left to serve in Vietnam.

Tom Conway had shoeboxes full of miniature green plastic army men. It seemed that whenever he missed his father, the sergeant, his mother would bring him home another bag of them. He had plastic tanks and jeeps, too. And a truck for transporting troops. One inch tall, these molded men were frozen in action: rifles pointed, bazookas held, grenades about to be tossed.

That summer Scotty and Tom played war most days. They traded off who got to be the United States. They moved the army men to their liking. A pretend explosion often ended the day's fighting. One boy would knock over the other boy's men—"Boom!" they would say.

Then, as they licked cherry and orange Popsicles, Scotty and Tom often discussed their fathers' war experiences.

"My dad's in Vietnam," Tom bragged. "He's killing people."

"So?"

"My dad kills people every day."

"Yeah, my dad killed people, too."

(The Judge had driven a jeep in World War II and worked in counterintelligence during the Korean War.)

"How many? My dad kills tons of people."

"My dad killed a lot of 'em, too."

"Liar."

"Am not."

"Liar!"

"Am not!"

The same thing usually happened: Scotty and Tom would fall on each other. Tom would run inside, his nose or some other part of him bloody, and Scotty, arms scraped, knees skinned, would walk home and wait for his mother to come driving up the street in her yellow convertible. Then he would tell his mother how he hated Tom Conway.

"Guess what I think, Scotty?" Joan asked once from inside her car. Her sunglasses were large and oval; her hair was pulled back with a light blue scarf. She had returned from a day of painting, and she smelled of cigarette smoke and turpentine.

"I think you're mad at *me,* not Tom Conway. . . ."

Scotty climbed over the car door and into the passenger seat.

"You take it out on Tom. But I'm the one who leaves you with them. You're *mad* at me."

"No," Scotty said. This was unthinkable.

"Scotty, it's all right if you are. I have so much painting to do."

"I'm not mad at you!"

Joan smiled and turned the car into the driveway. "Yes, you are, and it's all right."

"I'M NOT MAD!"

Those days when Joan let Scotty join her at her studio, he would stand nearby, painting and scribbling on blank sheets of paper clipped to his own miniature easel. If Joan needed to be alone for a while, Scotty would play in the parking lot, studying the movements of the ant colonies that had formed in the cracks of the concrete.

Armed with a dime or a handful of pennies, he walked alone to the drugstore where he picked out his favorite candy: Hot Dog bubble gum, Sweetarts, and square, light-brown Kraft caramels in individual plastic wrappers.

For lunch she took him to Anjo's Restaurant where he sucked up spaghetti one noodle at a time, leaving a ring of tomato sauce around his lips.

But mostly Scotty watched while Joan painted and smoked and drank.

That August during a hot spell, Scotty drew a picture of his parents. First he outlined his interpretation of Joan. He gave her yellow hair, a cigarette in her sticklike hand, and dressed her in a large shirt, which he colored with dots as if splattered with paint.

Joan said, "I bet I know who that is." Then, while Joan busied herself stretching a canvas, Scotty sketched his version of the Judge: a mass of limbs, a thick neck, and a large, looming body. He stopped when it came time to draw the Judge's face. He sat for a time and tried to picture the details. But as hard as he'd tried to imagine it, the Judge's face was a blur, so he left it blank.

It was the Judge's hands that Scotty could picture clearest— a Masonic ring on his right hand, a gold wedding band on the left, hairy knuckles—hands so huge the Judge could palm a basketball with ease, maybe even a globe, the textured kind.

Fingers so long that they could stretch over Scotty's eyes and ears, a grip so strong that if the Judge wanted he could crush Scotty's skull with a single squeeze.

This is what Scotty believed.

In late evenings, as the sun set, the Judge would stand with Scotty in front of the garage door, extend his hands and shape them in various ways, casting shadows of various animals. He'd already taught Scotty the rabbit, the snail, and the alligator. The Judge told Scotty to keep practicing. "And then," he said, "at parties you can be the entertainment."

In the finished sketch, the figure of the Judge covered the page, from top to bottom—he was two and a half times the size of Joan.

"Your dad isn't that big, Scotty."

"No?"

"Oh no," Joan said. "You got the proportions all wrong. He's maybe half as big as your drawing suggests."

"Oh."

Joan handed Scotty a pink eraser.

"Try again."

Scotty erased his father and tried again. He showed her the finished drawing.

"Very good, Scotty. You've cut him down to size."

(4)

Near the end of August, a moving van pulled up next door. Scotty happened to be climbing the larger willow tree at the time. With his hands and hair flecked with bark and leaves, he dropped to the ground and was the first of the neighbor kids to stand and watch the movers unload. Others arrived on bikes and roller skates or by foot and looked on as boxes were carried down the moving-van ramp. Everyone watching hoped to get a preview of the new family and what kind of people they would be.

Looking for clues, Scotty decided. Evidence.

First off were a series of boxes, then a bed frame wrapped in moving blankets, then an office desk.

"I see a bike," Scotty called out.

As the movers unloaded it, Scotty couldn't believe what he saw. Every boy's dream—a Schwinn five-speed, a big black knob for a gearshift, positioned like the stick shift in Joan's convertible, a banana seat with a large "S" for Schwinn, butterfly handlebars, hand brakes, a small front wheel with a coil-like spring below the handlebars to absorb bumps. With its blood-red bike frame, this particular model was called the Apple Krate.

There was no better bike than the bike of his new neighbor.

Scotty knew the boy would immediately be popular. And Scotty said to himself, "I'm going to be this person's friend."

All day Scotty waited in the yard, tugging at low-hanging branches, grabbing the seedling balls from the sycamore tree, breaking them open with his fingers, letting the insides scatter. Finally, when the neighbor's garage door was raised open, Scotty was waiting. He peered around a tree and watched as his new neighbor wheeled out his bike.

The neighbor stood the bike on its handlebars. He spun the wheel to check the alignment. He tested the brakes.

Scotty had never seen a boy quite like this.

The new boy looked as if he'd been stretched on one of those medieval torture racks. His long, skinny neck was like taffy. A prominent bump in his throat resembled a fist. His hair, buzzed short, stood up square on his head. Black and prickly, the new neighbor's hair must feel, Scotty decided, like a dog brush.

Scotty watched as the neighbor took playing cards from a deck and secured them with clothespins to the fender. Then he grunted, turned his bike over, straddled it, and pedaled off. As he rode, the bike spokes striking the playing cards made a machine gun sound.

Scotty's plan was to give a tour. Tips and pointers for the new neighbor. Highlights and information and history any new kid would want to know.

He'd show him the best hill for bikes, and the creek at the bottom of the street, below Pleasant Street, where the rain emptied and which ran parallel to Interstate 235. He'd show him the hill over on Twenty-first Street where Claire and Maggie had taken him the previous winter for sledding. He'd teach him to recognize the sound of the ice cream man.

He'd point out the empty lot on Twenty-second Street where a gang of future fourth graders made a ramp out of scrap wood, and where each day in the summer, after the construction workers had gone home, kids rode in circles, popping wheelies, smoothing out a trail around where the house was being built.

If it rained, Scotty could show him how he and Tom Conway and sometimes Tom Conway's sister Donna raced used Popsicle sticks in the rapids that formed on the sides of

Twenty-third Street after a thunderstorm. They'd race all the way past the Oceans' house, past the Conways', past the Sheltons' and the Foxes' and the Deubens', down to the sewer opening where water left the street and went underground. Wiffle balls, baseballs, the occasional Super Ball, rolled into the sewer, usually lost, unless, of course, a group of boys used a metal pipe or tree branch to lift off the sewer lid and someone dropped down to retrieve it.

What else? What else?

He decided to tell his neighbor everything he knew.

But there was the question of approach. How do I talk to him when he's so tall? When he has the best bike?

Scotty worried about these things as he stood alone in his yard. He didn't even know the neighbor boy's name. It would be days before he was to hear it. It was Claire who would make the announcement. "His name is Andrew Crow," she told her family. "He's in my math class." Then she repeated his last name, spelled it, and said, "Crow, like the pesky bird." She stabbed her fork into a pork chop. "An odd name," she went on to say. "For an odd boy."

(5)

They went kiss kiss on the front porch; then Joan waved as Scotty headed off, day one of second grade. He walked backward for a time, waving to his mom, her hair still messy from sleep.

Earlier, while tying Scotty's shoes for him, Joan told Scotty that he was going to have to learn to do this by himself.

"Okay," Scotty had promised, secretly planning never to learn shoe tying. Why should I, he thought, when my mom is so good at it?

Claire had left earlier, riding her bike the almost two miles to West Glen Junior High. Scotty was to walk with Maggie, who with her long, bony legs was already a house ahead of him when she called back, "Come on, Scotty, we're going to be late." He turned and ran to catch up with her. When he got close, he looked back and waved to his mom again. She was still there, still waving, but with a lit cigarette in her hand.

"Scotty, come on."

As he ran, he squeezed the ridges of the green plastic handle on his *Bonanza* lunch pail.

Except for the lunch pail (a holdover from first grade), everything about Scotty was new. His new book bag was filled with new items: large pencils called Husky, two Big Chief tablets, a box of forty-eight Crayola crayons, scissors with green handles and LEFTY stamped on the side, a pink rectangular eraser, a wooden ruler (with no teeth marks yet)—everything was new.

Even his clothes had never been worn before. The tags had been yanked off the night before. His polyester shirt itched; the collar pinched—"It's too small," Joan had said during shopping at Sears.

"No," Scotty said.

"You should wear a size eight, Scotty," she insisted.

"No."

"You're going to have to wear size eight eventually."

"No," Scotty said. "I hate eight."

His new Buster Brown shoes were shiny and roomy enough that he could wiggle his toes. At home, his new Keds tennis shoes waited to be worn after school and on weekends.

At the top of Woodland Street, Tom Conway stood dressed in his first-day-of-school outfit. He asked Scotty if he could walk with him.

Before Scotty could answer, Maggie said, "Sure, Tom, you can walk with us."

For Scotty, Maggie, and Tom Conway, it was a short walk to Clover Hills Elementary—up one street and down another. Others lived farther away and cars full of nervous kids and relieved parents zipped past that first day.

Carole Staley rode in the front as her father, a banker, drove her to school. With her dishwater-blond hair and green eyes pressed to the glass, Carole Staley called out the names of the kids she knew. "That's Lucy Titman. That's Leann Callahan."

But when she saw Scotty Ocean walking with his sister and Tom Conway, she didn't call out Scotty's name. She pressed her face to the window glass, her lips especially, and the car passed him.

"Carole, what are you doing?"

She quickly faced front, her lips having left a wet mark on the car window.

"Uhm," Carole said. "I don't know."

But she knew. Scotty Ocean had been her favorite boy in first grade. And now they would be in the same section in second grade. She had waited all summer for this day.

It was in front of Cindy McCameron's house that one of Scotty's shoes came untied.

"Maggie," Scotty said.

"What?"

Scotty pointed to his untied shoe.

"You do it yourself."

"Can't. Don't know how."

"Not my problem," said Maggie and she walked on.

"But . . ."

"I'm not Mom," Maggie snapped.

Scotty stopped and waited. He wouldn't budge.

The McCamerons had a swimming pool in their backyard. The blue slide could be seen poking above the wooden fence. In the winter, a rubber bubble would be filled with air, "winterizing" the pool, and Cindy had pool parties to which boys were never invited.

On certain breezy days, one could smell the chlorine from the water. On the hottest of days, one could hear kids splashing and playing from behind the fence. Sometimes neighbor kids would stand in the street and watch as little figures appeared at the top of the slide and then disappeared from view as they slid, a moment of nothingness until the inevitable splash and ensuing yelps.

Scotty turned and saw that Maggie was two houses away. He stared down at his untied shoe.

Tom Conway had waited. Tom said, "I can do it."

Knowing that Maggie wasn't going to come back to help, Scotty sighed. "Okay, but fast."

Tom, his hands shaking, his face looking serious, started to tie Scotty's shoe as best he could.

Thwap. Thwap. Thwap. Scotty froze when he heard it. He turned in time to see Andrew Crow approaching on his Schwinn five-speed, the playing cards rattling out his warning, on his way to West Glen Junior High.

Tom Conway didn't like Andrew Crow. "He's creepy," he would later say.

Andrew coasted by, his hands behind his head. He looked over at Scotty and laughed, a cackle of sorts. Scotty looked down and saw Tom Conway making the final loop in his shoelace. Pulling away his foot, undoing all of Tom's handiwork, Scotty said, "Forget it."

Andrew coasted down the street, finally disappearing with an upper body lean, turning his bike at Vine Street, using no hands to steer.

And Scotty thought, I wish I could do that.

"You ruined it," Tom said meekly.

"Tough," said Scotty and they walked on, Scotty's shoelace flailing with every other step.

When Scotty arrived at his new classroom with Tom Conway tagging along, Mrs. Boyden was standing in the doorway, staring at her watch. She looked up and said, "Good morning, I'm Mrs. Boyden. Please hurry and take your seat."

Each desk had a name tag taped in front.

Second grade meant each student got his own desk with a shelf. In first grade, four students shared a table. Third grade desks would have lids.

Scotty found his desk quickly. It was the third desk in the third row—he was sitting smack in the middle. Scotty looked around. Most of the kids he knew. Dan Burkhett and Craig Hunt were seated nearby. In the far corner, Jimmy Lamson sat wearing a blue suit coat and a red tie.

Scotty scanned the room. This is where he was to learn. In a far corner, near a large porcelain sink, a rack of hooks, waist high on adults, anticipated winter coats and scarves. In another corner, low shelves overflowed with books of all sizes. On top, a textured globe of the world waited to be spun. Near the classroom entrance, there was a pencil sharpener; a gray metal wastebasket; and a clock with a big face, easy-to-read numbers, and a red second hand that moved slowly. The speaker for the intercom system was secured to the wall, and an American flag extended at an angle from a metal holder. A fresh coat of beige paint had been applied to Mrs. Boyden's classroom over the summer. Above the blackboard, the alphabet printed in large letters ran the length of the room. Each letter appeared twice— the first time in capitals, the second in lower case. On the blackboard was written in block print: WELCOME.

Mrs. Boyden started the morning by introducing herself. She informed her class that she'd been teaching for over thirty-five years. "So," she said, "I know a thing or two."

Then she explained that every day there would be certain procedures. Roll taking, the Pledge of Allegiance, a morning and an afternoon recess *if you're good.*

"Why do we take attendance, class?" She paused and then answered her own question. "So we know if you're here."

Scotty listened as Mrs. Boyden read the names of her new students. She appeared to be in no hurry. She explained that she preferred it if each person would answer by saying, "Present." For it was no great feat for any of the students to be "here." "Your parents made sure you were here. But to be 'present,' that is an accomplishment."

As Mrs. Boyden spoke, she'd look at a student, sneak a quick glance at his or her tag, and make a mental note that linked the face to the name. "Everyone likes to be known by their name," she believed. And in thirty-five years of first days, she had never failed—she always knew each of their names by the end of the day.

"Scott Ocean?"

Scotty said nothing.

"Scott?"

She looked around the room, squinting as she searched for him.

Scotty slowly raised his hand. "I am Scotty."

Mrs. Boyden made a mental note of his name. "You're the brother of Claire and Maggie?"

"Yes, ma'am."

"I was their teacher."

"You were?"

"Didn't they tell you?"

"Yes."

"I want to say something to you, Scotty. Your sisters were special students, two of my favorites. It would be unfair of me to expect you to be like them. Wouldn't it?"

"Uhm," Scotty said.

"I think it would."

Scotty felt everyone looking at him.

Mrs. Boyden smiled. "I want you to be you. I want you to be yourself."

Mrs. Boyden knew of the dangers of sibling comparison. Claire Ocean had been the brightest, most curious student in Mrs. Boyden's experience. Though not as bright, Maggie was sweet and lovely, and a beauty-to-be. "I won't be comparing you," Mrs. Boyden said.

Scotty smiled because she seemed to want him to.

"Of course," Mrs. Boyden continued, "if you're anything like your sisters, that would be nice. There is much to admire about them."

Mrs. Boyden's glasses were horn-rimmed, the frame a milky gray color. She looked large, with strong, thick arms, and when she turned around, Scotty saw purple blotches, grape jelly–like strands, colored lightning down the backs of her legs. Her age, he thought, was easy to guess. She was close to a hundred.

"Yep," he said at dinner. "She's a hundred. At least."

His sisters laughed, for they knew she was in no way that age. "She looks old, but she's not that old," Claire announced.

Scotty sipped at his milk.

The girls had made a dinner of individual pot pies, which they heated in the oven. The Judge went to Kiwanis on Wednesdays and Joan was painting at her studio.

"She's working on her show," Claire said.

Joan would be displaying a series of new paintings at the end of the month.

"She's painting all the time," Scotty moaned.

"That's what artists do."

Scotty said, "I know that!"

When the Judge returned home, it was past their bedtime. He shooed them upstairs to bed.

"Where's Mom?" Scotty asked.

The Judge said, "She's painting. On to bed everyone."

And up the girls went. Scotty lingered. He wanted the Judge to carry him to bed.

"You're a second grader now, Scotty. Go on by yourself."

Scotty sighed and climbed the stairs alone.

(6)

With the first week of classes out of the way, and having established the class rules and procedures, Mrs. Boyden felt that they could finally get around to the business of learning. So early on Monday of the second week, she asked her students, "What do we all have in common?" She paused. "What about us is *the same?*"

Ruth Rethman raised her hand and said, "We all have hair."

"Yes, Ruth, we all have hair in common."

Carole Staley, tall for her age, her hair in pigtails, raised her hand.

"Mrs. Boyden? My dad doesn't. He's bald."

Mrs. Boyden clarified: "Carole, I'm talking about all of us in this room. Look around. What do all of us *in this room* have in common?"

While she waited for more answers, Mrs. Boyden turned and wrote "hair" on the chalkboard. "What else?"

They began to call out their ideas and Mrs. Boyden compiled a list.

Eyes. Nose. Feet. Toes.

"Very good, everyone."

Shoes. Clothes. Teeth.

"Very, very good!"

"We're all seven," Scotty called out.

"I'm not!" Craig Hunt shouted. Craig was eight. He'd been held back. He would be nine in March.

"And I won't be for long," Dan Burkhett added. Dan Burkhett's birthday was less than two weeks away.

"So we're not all seven. Anyone else?"

"Pets," Cindy McCameron suggested.

"Does everyone have a pet?"

A disappointed Tom Conway slowly raised his hand. "Not me," he said.

"If we don't all have pets, then we don't have that in common."

Bev Fowler said, "We all have moms."

"That's right. You all have moms. And dads. Let's not forget dads. Even I have a mom and dad," Mrs. Boyden added, "and I'm old enough to be your grandmother. Both of my parents are still alive."

Every so often Mrs. Boyden let a personal revelation slip out. Sometimes she forgot that she was talking to second graders. Usually, though, their lack of response snapped her back into reality, reminding her that the people in front of her were children.

"Can anyone think of anything else we have in common?"

There was a silence.

"Anyone?"

Mrs. Boyden had written so much she had to take out a new piece of chalk, which, when she wasn't writing, she held like a cigarette.

"I'm looking for an answer that I suspect none of you will have."

No room remained on the chalkboard so Mrs. Boyden took an eraser and rubbed a large circular area clean. With her back to them, she wrote in large, thick block lettering, "IOWANS."

Mrs. Boyden asked, "What does that mean?"

No one knew.

"It means we're from Iowa."

Over the next several days, she would teach them the the state bird (goldfinch), the state rock (geode), the state flower (goldenrod), and the state song, which on special days they would sing after saying the Pledge of Allegiance. She would tell them about the many famous Iowans—John Wayne was from Winterset, Johnny Carson had been born over near Council Bluffs, and Herbert Hoover, the thirty-first President of the United States, was born and now was buried in West Branch. This intense study of "the Corn State" would culminate with a trip to the Iowa Historical Society early in October.

But it was always on the first day she taught Iowa that Mrs. Boyden said and did the following:

"Three quarters of the earth is covered by water; there are five continents, hundreds of countries (including America), and fifty states, of which Iowa is one."

She pulled down a map of the United States. Each state was a different color.

"Who can find Iowa?"

Before any of her students could volunteer, Mrs. Boyden had taken her pointer stick and tapped the map.

"Here. Here it is."

Scotty and his classmates looked intently at the small state in the middle.

"Iowa," she said with relish, "is where we all are."

(7)

"You couldn't ask for better weather," the Judge said as he turned the Dodge into the first parking space he saw. The sky was cloudless and the air warm for late September. "This is probably the last day a person will be able to wear short sleeves." Scotty and his sisters got out of the car as fast as they could.

It had been a few days since they had seen Joan. Every year

she worked in a fury to finish in time, but this year she had worked extra-long hours because, as she explained to them, "my work has gone in a new direction."

The crowd of people who attended Joan's art show consisted of friends, members of the church, the Judge's secretary, Judge Frohn and his wife, the baker Jerry Magill and his wife, and—to Joan's satisfaction—a number of people she didn't know.

She had everyone gather in the parking lot outside of her studio, and Joan, dressed in a floral skirt and a black blouse, stood in front of the door. She normally let the work speak for itself and allowed people to wander in and out. But for this show, she wanted to be more formal. She wanted to urge the first-timers to sign her mailing list. Most important, she wanted to prepare people for what they were about to see.

"I want to welcome you to my show. And in advance, I want to thank you for your support. It means so much."

Claire whispered to Maggie, "Mom's nervous."

Joan wanted to explain her new approach. But she couldn't think of the right way to explain the unexplainable, so she finished by saying, "I hope you like what you see." Then she stepped out of the way. Scotty darted in front of the others, for he wanted to be the first inside.

The studio was spotless. Her supplies were packed away in the coat closet and in boxes on shelves in the bathroom. She removed anything that would distract from the ten large canvases that hung on the walls. These paintings were unlike anything Joan had ever made before.

Each painting was a variation on a theme: Joan naked. Joan lying down. Joan sitting with her legs crossed. Joan smoking. Joan clenching a fist. Joan asleep. In all of them Joan was naked.

She hadn't flattered herself. In fact, it was as if she had gone out of her way to distort herself. The Judge's first impulse was to say, "She's much prettier than this." But he said nothing. As he glanced from painting to painting, he wondered, Why would a person make themselves less appealing than they are?

All ten paintings were done in oil. In some cases, and not because of haste, Joan left large globs on the canvas. That gave a texture to the work: the impression that these paintings had been carved.

At one end of the studio, a folding table served as a place to get refreshments: bottles of pop, wine, platters of cheese and crackers, a plate of celery and carrot sticks.

Joan had asked Claire and Maggie to serve refreshments. Scotty had the run of the place.

"Mom's in a rut," Claire whispered to Maggie during a lull in their serving.

Scotty came over. He wanted to know what she had said.

"It's nothing, Scotty. Anyway, Dad wants you outside."

Scotty ran on.

"Yep," Maggie said. "Mom's in a rut."

Outside, the Judge talked with a lawyer acquaintance. They discussed politics, football, and a recent Supreme Court decision—everything but Joan's paintings. He had supported her by buying the supplies, the paint, but he knew he would have to say something soon. He couldn't afford to spend money in this manner. He wouldn't mention it now, but soon he'd have to say something.

For Joan, this new work was brave and honest, her best ever. But she could tell by the quick manner in which the guests moved through her studio; she could tell by their sometimes blank, sometimes confused faces and the way they struggled to find nice words that they did not approve. And then, an hour into her reception, the simple fact that almost everyone was outside, smoking and talking about other things, indicated to Joan that nothing was going to sell.

So she taped up several of Scotty's watercolors on a bare section of wall and called for the guests to gather around. She started to auction Scotty's paintings and a kind person, a hippielike man who wore a colorful tie, bid five dollars for all six paintings.

"Sold," Joan said.

She gave Scotty the five dollars and said, "When you get paid, Scotty, it makes you a professional." Then she told him to go home with his father and sisters. Scotty wanted to stay with Joan, but she said that she'd clean up and be home soon after.

(8)

The day after the art show, Scotty spent the afternoon with his mother watching TV. He curled up with her on the sofa. He told her about all he had been learning at school. "The gold-finch is the state bird," he said. But he'd already forgotten the state rock and the state flower. Joan said, "It's okay, sweetie. There are more important things to remember."

Then she sent him to the basement. He moved fast. He loved to be helpful.

Standing before his mother, Scotty held the can proudly. He peeled off the tab in one swift move. The beer foamed and ran over the sides. Joan took the can, her mouth open, and used her tongue and lips to catch the beer. Some of it got on Scotty's fingers so she licked them, too.

There was none of her usual embarrassment as this was

already her fourth can. Scotty had been bringing her beers since early that afternoon, the first one arriving minutes after the Judge took Claire and Maggie to the Merle Hay Shopping Center.

After each empty can, Scotty would wash it out carefully in the sink, go to the garage and step on it, crushing it into a metal pancake, and put it in a hidden sack behind Joan Ocean's garden tools. The sack was filled with secret cans. One day soon they would drive to the Dumpster behind Kmart and throw the cans away.

Back in the house, Scotty unwrapped a stick of his mother's gum. She opened her mouth and he slid it between her lips. "This will make mother's breath beautiful," she said. Then she told him how much she loved him. "And, Scotty, remember— you're my favorite son."

"But I'm your only son."

"All the more reason."

Later she was to say, "Mother needs a nap."

Standing in front of her, though, book in one hand, a pen in the other, was Scotty. She looked with surprise at her young man.

She extended her arms and pulled him tight to her chest. He wiggled free enough to hold up the book. He hoped he was clear.

"Didn't we just do this a few weeks back?"

"I know," he said. "But I'm growing fast. A spurt."

"Nobody grows that fast."

"I do. At night, I can hear my bones stretching, creaking and things. You can hear me growing, too, if you listen." He held an arm up to her ear.

"Scotty, later, okay? We'll do it later."

"MEASURE ME. MEASURE ME NOW!"

. . .

Joan Ocean finished a fifth beer before measuring Scotty for the final time. Holding the book proved nearly impossible. She dropped it twice, which she found hysterically funny. Scotty joined her, imitating her laugh and stomping the floor in an identical way.

"Stretch even higher," she told him. "One day you'll be taller than everybody, taller than your father."

Scotty yelled, "Yes!" rose on tiptoe with his shoes still on, as Joan drew the straightest line she could.

Afterward, as he stood admiring his new height, he heard a strange sound, a mixture of hacking and gagging, and thought *My mom is dying.* He ran down the hallway to Joan, who was down on all fours, the final webs of vomit strung out her mouth.

He tried to wipe up the mess. Then he helped her to bed where he washed her face with a wet washcloth.

"Scotty is growing," she said, before falling off to sleep. "Look at Scotty grow."

(9)

Apart from Craig Hunt, Dan Burkhett was the first of Scotty's friends to turn eight. For his party, Dan invited only boys from his class. He started the celebration by opening his gifts. As he tore off the first handful of wrapping paper, he said, in a matter-of-fact tone, "Eight is great."

Dan Burkhett's mother smiled. She had hair like a grandmother, gray and white, but her face was young and sweet with thin creases around her eyes when she smiled. She never raised her voice. As the librarian at West Glen Junior High, she always spoke in a whisper—even, it was said, while cheering at the University of Nebraska football games. Her husband, Jerry, had been the punter for the team in the early 1950s. Jerry Burkhett, a proud trustee for the university, outfitted his kids with University of Nebraska jerseys, T-shirts, caps, and key rings. Around their home the favorite phrase was "Go Big Red." Jerry Burkhett spent his weekends during football season kicking footballs high in the air. He had a nylon bag full of ten or twelve footballs. The Burkhetts lived next door to an empty lot.

For Dan's eighth birthday, his mom brought out a plate of Rice Krispie treats, a gallon of milk, and Nestlé's Quik. The backyard was full of yellow and orange and brown leaves, and the boys, in sweaters and sweatshirts, made crunching noises when they ran. Jerry Burkhett emerged from the tool shed with his nylon bag of footballs. Dan Burkhett's friends, Scotty included, spread out over the empty lot.

Jerry Burkhett began booting footballs, kicking an occasional spiral, but usually end-over-end spins. The boys would yell, "I got it!" Then they would run under the ball, and always, at the last second, let the ball bounce on the ground.

"Come on, boys. Be men. Is there a man among you!" Jerry Burkhett shouted.

Then Dan positioned himself under a ball that sailed above him. While he was trying to catch it, the football bulleted into his chest. The wind knocked out of him, Dan buckled over.

Evidence enough, Scotty thought. Eight wasn't so great.

Dan's mom ran out to him and hugged him and whispered things into his ear and suddenly the party was over.

Had he dreamt it? Scotty didn't know, but when he woke up the day after Dan Burkhett's party, he had a vague memory of his mother climbing in bed with him, her beer breath, her crying and him patting her back and saying, "It's okay." Over and over he said it, "It's okay." That is what he was trying to remember as Claire stood over his bed, poking him with her pointer finger. She'd been trying to wake him for some time.

"Scotty, Dad wants us in the living room."

Scotty was slow to rise, and Claire pulled him by the wrist, and said it was urgent.

"Ow," Scotty said, as he sleepily made his way down the hall, thudded down the stairs into the living room where Maggie sat in the sofa waiting, her back rigid, like a teen model. She didn't look at Scotty.

Claire shouted out, "Dad, Scotty's up."

"One minute," the Judge called from the bathroom.

Scotty crossed to the TV. Tom and Jerry cartoons on a Sunday morning.

"No TV," Claire said.

Scotty pushed the "on" button anyway.

Claire lunged to the TV and turned it off. "No, Scotty," she said.

He looked to Maggie for support but she seemed lost in thought. Something was wrong. The muted sound of the downstairs toilet being flushed jumped in volume as the Judge swung open the bathroom door. He walked down the hall and stood in the living room. He was dressed for church. He straddled a wooden chair that had been brought in from the kitchen. He looked at all three children and tried to smile. But his empty eyes didn't agree with his mouth, and the smile had a forced quality. Claire thought it looked phony. "Wipe that smile off your face!" Maggie wanted to shout.

Claire sat in the middle of the sofa, an arm draped over Maggie's shoulder and a hand resting on Scotty's knee. Scotty's feet dangled off the sofa and he thought, One day my feet will touch.

The Judge took in a breath and sighed. "I know you all must be worried about your mother."

He'd only said the "m" in mother when Maggie started to cry. Claire tried to calm her. The Judge asked Maggie to please stop. "We're upset," Claire said, "and don't expect us to be all smiles."

"Of course," the Judge said.

Maggie said, "You got to tell us where she went, Daddy."

The Judge stopped smiling.

Scotty calmly asked, "Where's Mom?"

The Judge paused.

"Where's Mom?" Scotty repeated.

"I don't know."

And the Judge didn't know. He only knew she was gone and that earlier, while he was on the toilet reading the paper, he had heard a noise. He flipped on the porch light and Joan turned like a deer frozen in headlights. A small suitcase in hand, she was packing up her car.

"What the hell . . . ?"

Joan shrugged as if she might start laughing, and said, "There's a note on the kitchen table." Then she climbed in her yellow convertible and drove away.

The Judge headed to the kitchen. He opened the envelope, which read, "Walter." He unfolded the paper. Written in Joan's hand, her cursive that flowed and circled and looped, was one word—"Good-bye."

Other sealed envelopes—thicker, more pages—had been left for the children. Holding Claire's letter up to the light, the Judge saw words, whole sentences even. The children got explanations, but he only got one word.

He tore open Claire's letter. Words like "diminished" and "inevitable." In Maggie's, Joan advised her not to hurry with boys—that if she chose too quickly, she might regret—and there was nothing worse than regret. In her note to Scotty, she had made a drawing of a boy and his mother holding hands. She wrote that there would be between them, always, a love, and then she kissed the paper, leaving her lipstick lips. Both girls were told to look after Scotty, because to be a boy in a house full of big sisters was no easy thing. Each letter was signed, "Love, Mom."

The Judge sat motionless and tried to figure out what to do. Stunned, he hid the notes in the sugar bowl and waited until it was time to wake the children.

He could think of no nice way to tell them.

"Why?" Claire kept asking.

"The pressures. Worry. I don't know."

"Did you do something to her?"

"No, of course not," the Judge said.

"Why did she leave?"

Scotty sat quietly. He had an idea why.

"What we have to do is pull ourselves together. If she calls, tell her you miss her, but tell her we're fine."

Claire said, "Are you telling us what to say?"

"I'm making a suggestion."

"I hate it when you tell us what to say!"

The Judge was flustered.

"You don't know why she left!" Claire shouted.

Maggie held her face in her hands. Her crying sounded like she was laughing.

And Scotty said, "Where did she go?"

"She's going to miss us. You watch, she'll be back soon. She just needs some time."

Maggie stopped crying. "Why, Daddy?"

Scotty started to slap at his head.

"Listen, kids—I'm suggesting that we pull ourselves together. Scotty, stop it."

Scotty continued his slapping.

"She'll miss us because she'll know we're having all the . . . uhm . . . fun."

"Fun!" Claire shouted. Maggie wailed. Scotty slapped his head harder. Claire stormed out of the house, letting the screen door slam. And the Judge thought, Bad word choice, fun.

"Come back," the Judge said loudly. "Claire, come back here!"

Claire continued up the street and Maggie wedged her face between the sofa cushions, muting her sounds. As the Judge sighed, Scotty felt the facts sink in. His mom was gone. And he knew why.

A GOOD BOY

(1)

Even though the Judge had no culinary skills, he took over the cooking. Several days were needed to gather recipes from Marjorie, his secretary, and other workers at the courthouse, so during the first week, he took the children to an assortment of restaurants: Shakey's Pizza, Sambo's, and McDonald's twice. By mid-October, a simple menu could be managed, and while most foods were overcooked, the Judge succeeded in making meals his children would eat.

And it was during those first days that the Judge took his children to the movies. In the two weeks after Joan left, they would see nine: first, Dick Van Dyke in *Some Kind of a Nut* at the Ingersoll Theater, then Julie Andrews in *Those Were the Happy Times* at the Plaza. That Saturday he dropped them off at the special kiddie matinee at the Wakonda, where for seventy-five cents, they saw *The Three Stooges in Orbit* and *Clarence, the Cross-Eyed Lion*. Claire and Maggie disliked the kiddie matinee, but Claire understood that the Judge had work to do. *Doctor Dolittle* was revived at the Varsity and the Plaza brought back *Darby O'Gill and the Little People,* which Scotty especially liked. Claire begged to see *Change of Habit* at the Pioneer drive-in, arguing "They say it's the first good movie Elvis has made." But the Judge didn't think a drive-in a good idea. It was getting cold at night.

At the Galaxy they saw *One Hundred and One Dalmatians.* The best movie ever, Scotty announced. Until the next day when he saw *The Computer Wore Tennis Shoes,* which then became the best movie ever. Maggie said they all can't be the best, and Claire stepped on Maggie's foot to silence her. And then they waited for the Judge to drive up in the Dodge.

But Scotty knew the two he liked best, better than any other movies ever made—*The Battle of Britain* and *Tora! Tora! Tora!*—which they saw on successive Saturdays at the River Hill Theater, Des Moines's finest movie house. These were great movies, bloody and loud.

However, the experience of watching these two war movies left the girl Oceans embittered.

"Surely we could see something other than war movies."

"Surely there is something other . . ."

Then the frequency of moviegoing slowed. Scotty believed it was because of his sisters' complaints, but the truth was the Judge had taken them to every movie in the Des Moines area that was suitable for family viewing.

At home, much television was watched. The Judge made nightly bowls of popcorn, and during commercial breaks he would play the piano. Scotty requested a bouncy song called "Alley Cat," which the Judge played with enthusiasm. Once was fine, but after six or seven times, Maggie complained, "Daddy, learn another song."

The Judge believed that if he could keep the family occupied, Joan would come to her senses and return. If she drove by at night and looked in the window, she would see that the Ocean house was the place to be.

One night while supper was cooking, the Judge entered the living room and said he had an idea for an activity. He held a book in one hand, a pen in the other. "Who wants to go first?"

Claire did, then Maggie.

"Both of you have grown," the Judge said.

They looked at their new heights. Claire said she hadn't needed the measurement to confirm what she'd already felt— she was taller. Maggie wasn't interested in growing taller—she dreamt of growing in other directions.

"Scotty?" the Judge called out.

"No thank you," he yelled back.

"Scotty, it's a family activity. I *insist*."

As Scotty stood with his back to the kitchen closet door, the Judge placed a book, one from Claire's Nancy Drew collection, on top of Scotty's head. "Aren't you forgetting something?" the Judge asked.

"Oh yeah," Scotty said, kicking off his shoes. As the Judge took a pen from his pocket, Scotty stretched as high as he could.

"Scotty's trying to cheat," said Maggie, who had been standing unnoticed by the refrigerator.

"No," Scotty barked.

"Is to. Tried to wear his shoes. Now he's standing on his toes. Scotty is a cheater!"

The Judge smiled. "There is nothing wrong, Maggie, with wanting to grow."

. . .

(Within weeks Maggie would begin stuffing concentrated amounts of Kleenex into a borrowed bra. Her father's words, having echoed in her head, would give her the needed permission.

In late February, while wandering around Kmart, Scotty would notice a tuft of tissue sticking out from Maggie's blouse. He'd approach her, pull on it while many people, mostly boys, watched. He'd hold the confiscated goods for all to see. Maggie would know then the feeling Scotty was having now. And she'd flinch when her own words returned to haunt: "Maggie is a cheater. Maggie is a cheater."

But that day was months away.)

So it was with great regret that Scotty Ocean stood his actual height. He listened to the sound of the Judge drawing the line above his head. The line was drawn in red ink.

Scotty stepped away and looked up. His new mark was two inches lower than his previous measurement, the one Joan had just taken.

"Well I'll be," the Judge said with suspicion. "Somebody's getting smaller."

At dinner, the Judge couldn't ignore Scotty, who sat with his head down. Yes, Scotty had been deceptive—and yes, he'd tried to distort his true height, and that wasn't to be encouraged. But enough was enough, and the Judge spoke: "My dear and very special children . . ."

The girls looked at the Judge. Maggie thought it queer that their dad spoke like a Bible.

He continued, "Do you know the effect of gravity?"

Scotty sat looking at his plate, searching for his reflection like the woman on the TV commercial.

Claire smiled a look of recognition: "We did a whole section on it."

"Tell us about gravity."

Claire said the word, spelled it, said it again.

"Correct," said the Judge.

"It's a pull. When you drop something, it falls down instead of up. It *gravitates*."

Maggie interjected, "Gravity keeps you from floating off into space."

Suddenly, Scotty rose up, floating above the table. He lay pressed to the ceiling. The others stared up at him, their mouths still slowly chewing. He crawled across the ceiling. He pushed open the front door with his forehead, sailed outside, got caught for a moment in the big sycamore tree, freed himself, and floated off as his family shouted, "Come back, come back!" The farther away he got, the smaller he grew. Scotty was gone.

He returned to the table as his father said, "Claire, that is correct. So Scotty, girls—gravity takes its effect on every one of us. How is this illustrated? The average man or woman is half an inch, sometimes a whole inch, shorter at the end of the day than he is at the beginning. And all because of . . ."

The Judge paused, and like the conductor of an orchestra, gestured for everyone to speak in unison.

"Gravity," they said.

"So," Maggie added, "you're saying Scotty came up short—"

"Yes, that's what he's saying," Claire said.

"I asked Dad."

The Judge put a hand in the air. Whenever he raised his hand, the children were to stop talking, even if they were in mid-sentence. But Maggie kept on with her comments, ranting about how Scotty had no right to cheat. The Judge snapped two fingers of his raised hand. Maggie continued talking. Without warning, he took his water glass, and with a swift, precise move, emptied it on Maggie, drenching her.

She stopped. Her bottom lip curled out, and she covered where her breasts would one day be. "Scotty was the cheater, Daddy. Not—" She stopped when she saw the Judge's hand in the air.

"In answer to your question," the Judge said, "I believe it is possible, due to gravity, for Scotty to come up shorter. We must consider the pull of the earth."

The Ocean girls had been excused. Maggie, all wet, left the table in tears; Claire followed to make it better.

The Judge and Scotty sat alone.

"There's a lot of good meat left on these bones."

Scotty watched his father pick at the food.

"A lot of good meat."

Scotty had lost his appetite.

"You do the dishes."

"Yes, sir."

Punished, good.

He took hours washing and drying each dish by hand. He put away the silverware and left the dishes on the counter for morning, when someone taller, the Judge most likely, would put them away.

The girls were asleep by the time Scotty finished, and in the living room, the Judge had nodded off while watching the late news. Scotty turned off the television, woke the Judge, and turned off the lights. He followed his dad up the stairs.

And as he climbed, Scotty contemplated his lifetime full of mistakes. If only I had done more of this, less of that, he thought.

And he made a mental list, indelibly scrawling it onto his heart. If only he hadn't used the kissing machine on her all those times. If only he hadn't done the seven dance, or licked the mailbox, then maybe she'd have stayed.

If only I wasn't such a cheater, he thought as he climbed into bed, the bed that was still hers.

(2)

Where was Joan?

That became a frequent question in the minds of many people. Periodically there would be a sighting—she'd be seen idling in her yellow convertible at a stoplight; Liz Conway saw her getting cigarettes out of a machine at Harold Drake's gas station. Once she was seen pushing an empty grocery cart down an aisle at the Safeway, laughing, no bra on, her breasts jiggling up and down, her laugh forced and unfortunate.

Rhonda Fowler called Brenda Burkhett and said, "You'll never believe who I just saw at Safeway . . ."

The Oceans went to church. They were Joan-less. The Judge told the children to say to anyone who asked that their mother wasn't feeling well. The Judge seemed stiffer, and the girls looked older suddenly, and Scotty didn't fidget. His behavior seemed impeccable. Someone mentioned that Joan had closed her gallery. Someone else heard she was staying on the other side of town.

(3)

After school when she knew the Judge wouldn't be home, Joan made a secret call to her kids.

"Let me talk to Scotty. Is Scotty on the phone? Scotty, are you there?"

"He's on," Maggie said.

"Scotty? Hello, little love."

"He's on. Talk!"

"Are you sure he's on?"

"I hear him breathing."

A faint "Hi."

"Was that you?"

A faint "Yes."

"Can you talk a little louder? For your mom? How are you?"

A faint "Good."

"You have to speak up. I'm calling from a pay phone. You know how pay phones are."

"Scotty, talk to Mom. You've been wanting to. He's always practicing what he wants to tell you. I have to listen to him all the way to school. He talks a mile a minute. And now you call and he says nothing. Come on, Scotty!"

"Honey, what are you doing?"

A faint "TV."

"What're you watching?"

"Nothing."

"I miss you so much." Joan dropped another coin in the phone. "You know that, don't you? Scotty?"

"I think he put down the phone, Mom, because I don't hear him breathing."

Scotty watched as Claire and Maggie, after hanging up the phone, began a frantic search. Claire checked the Judge's room, opening his sock drawer, his underwear drawer—Maggie checked the living room bookcase and sorted through the stack of papers in the kitchen.

"What are you doing?" Scotty asked.

"If you had stayed on the phone," Claire said, "you'd know exactly what we're looking for."

The more they searched, the angrier they became. So when the Judge entered the house, Claire and Maggie stood waiting, fuming.

"Where are they?" Claire asked.

The Judge looked puzzled.

"Mom said she wrote us letters."

"Where are they!" Maggie shouted.

"Oh," the Judge said.

"I can't believe it!"

"You keeping them from us, Dad?" Maggie said.

"I forgot," the Judge said. "Honest." He went to the sugar bowl and lifted the lid. "Here, kids."

He handed them their letters.

"You *read* them?" Claire said, referring to the torn envelopes. "I can't believe you read them!"

Claire and Maggie, letters in hand, stomped up the stairs.

"I'm sorry," the Judge said.

Scotty stood holding his letter. "It's okay, Dad."

"She might not be your wife," Claire shouted. "But she's still our mother!"

Later the Judge climbed the stairs. "Claire, Maggie," the Judge called from the hallway. "I'm sorry."

(4)

Whenever the family watched TV, Scotty crouched on the carpet, on his knees, ready to sprint. If the phone rang, Scotty was off and running. Living in a world dominated by his ten- and twelve-year-old sisters, he needed a head start. After all, it might be his mother calling, and if he was first, he'd have her all to himself, if only for a moment, and he could say what he wished he'd said when she called that one time—he'd say what he rehearsed, the magic words that would make her come back: "I'll be good."

Claire tried to answer Scotty's question. "They always say 'Please' and 'Thank you.' What else? Good boys are polite and clean and do what is required."

"Okay," Scotty said.

"But most important, good boys help with chores."

"Okay."

"Does that answer it?"

"Yep."

"They help with chores, Scotty." Then she said, "Hint, hint."

As Claire went to the basement, Scotty ran upstairs and gathered the dirty clothes. His arms full, he pushed the clothes through an opening and they dropped through the clothes chute. Claire was measuring out detergent when she heard the sound of clothes coming—the *whoosh*—and she stepped out of the way just in time as the clothes plopped on the floor.

"Scotty!"

He didn't hear her, for he was busy running down the two flights of stairs.

Scotty learned much about laundry in those first days. How to separate the whites from the colors. How to hold the glass measuring cup while Claire filled it with detergent.

"Something about laundry I love, Scotty."

"Yeah?"

"We choose our own hours."

"Yeah."

He learned about bleach and appropriate wash cycles and water temperatures. Claire reminded him of the dangers of a blue sock getting in a load of whites. He came to respect clothing and he felt important helping his sister—and he knew this was a benefit of having turned seven.

And when they finished a load, he'd beg Claire to compliment him. He'd keep begging until she said, "Good work." Or, "That was good." Anything with "good."

(5)

Carole Staley bragged to the class, "My mom's making my costume." She described how her mother was going to take a grocery sack, cut holes for the arms, make an elastic headband, and top it all off with a turkey feather. Then she told how her mom was going to paint red and blue streaks of "war" paint on her, thereby turning Carole into an authentic Indian princess.

"What are you going as?" she asked Scotty.

He shrugged. Usually Joan made him an elaborate costume. In kindergarten he had gone as a clown, and in first grade he went as the devil. But this year he didn't know. The Judge assured him that he could pick out any costume under a certain price range.

"You don't know what you're going to be?"

Scotty said nothing.

Carole offered to have her mother make a second costume and Scotty quickly said no.

Tom Conway said he would go as a wounded soldier. He planned to wrap his head in a cloth bandage and to use ketchup for blood.

Other kids had their plans—hobos, ghosts, ballerinas. A group of fourth graders were dressing up as the characters in *The Mod Squad*.

Scotty's store-bought costume was of an astronaut. The plastic mask was to be held in place by a rubber band, but on Halloween night as he stretched it out over his head, the rubber band broke.

"You'll be all right," the Judge said to a frustrated Scotty, who now would have to hold the mask in place using one hand.

Maggie wore torn overalls, covered her cheeks with charcoal, and went as a hobo. They both carried plastic pumpkins for gathering candy.

The Keiths gave caramel apples, the Biechlers gave popcorn balls, and Dr. Kovacs, a dentist, gave out toothbrushes. The best house for candy was that of Leann Callahan's grandparents, who lived on Vine Street. They gave adult-sized candy bars and after Scotty told his joke—"What's the biggest pen in the world? Pennsylvania"—the grandmother dropped a second candy bar into Scotty's plastic pumpkin.

Scotty had a favorite costume.

Andrew Crow had taken one of the boxes his family had used during their move. Using a scissors, he poked numerous holes equally spaced throughout the box. He threaded tiny Christmas lights through each hole and using a 9-volt battery, he made a space monster.

"A monster of the future," he announced to anyone who would listen.

Andrew had worked for weeks on his costume. Inside the cardboard were elastic straps that hung over his shoulders—these helped keep the box buoyant. A smaller box, head size, rested on top, and it was secured in such a way that he could turn his head separately from the body section of his robot. He punched out holes for eyes and put in a cheese grater for the mouth. When he spoke, he tried to speak with an electronic voice.

It was the best costume on the block.

Scotty wanted more than anything to get close to Andrew Crow. Every so often he could see, a few houses behind him, the blinking lights of Andrew Crow's costume approaching. Scotty would slow down as much as possible, but Maggie would invariably call for him to hurry up.

And if Scotty hesitated, she'd stretch out her hand, grab his, pull him along, and say, "You're slowing me down."

(6)

One November morning, after the class had recited the Pledge of Allegiance, Mrs. Boyden told her students to sit. Smiling, she said, "Now we're going to learn something useful." Then she hoisted a large box up onto her desk.

Scotty and the others wondered what was inside. Everyone sensed the importance of the day's teaching because Mrs. Boyden seemed particularly excited. Her voice had an unusual enthusiasm and that enthusiasm was contagious.

"We're going to learn something you will use every day."

Every day, Scotty thought.

"We're going to learn something you can use for the rest of your life."

"Oh, boy," Scotty said. Something had special value if you could use it for the rest of your life.

Mrs. Boyden held up a large plastic clock—tan with a white face and big black, easy-to-read numbers.

"You'll each get your own."

"Our own," whispered Scotty to himself.

She called the class forward by rows. As she handed each student a clock, she said, "Be careful."

Knobs in the back made it possible to turn the hands.

"These aren't real," Dan Burkhett whispered to Scotty. "They don't have a tick."

When Scotty got his, he held it to his ear. "No tick," he announced, as if he'd discovered it himself.

By midweek Mrs. Boyden could announce a time and in less than a minute her students would manipulate the knobs, turning the clock hands to point in the appropriate directions, and hold up their clocks victoriously. To Mrs. Boyden's pleasure, most of her students would have the big and little hands in the appropriate place.

"Very good."

And then she'd call out another time.

"Very good."

Mrs. Boyden knew how to teach the telling of time. She knew not to overwhelm the child with too much information. The following week she would explain A.M. and P.M. Later still would come time zones and phrases like "a quarter past," "half past," "a quarter to"—but for now they had learned enough.

At the end of class on Friday, Mrs. Boyden told her students she was proud of each and every one of them. It was good for everyone to feel satisfied on a Friday.

Scotty stayed practicing the telling of time after the bell

rang. The other kids put their chairs upside down on their desks and left the classroom. Scotty didn't see Carole Staley come up behind him. She placed her wet lips quickly on his right elbow, pulling away fast, leaving a ring of spit.

"Aagh," went Scotty as he rubbed his elbow. "Aagh!"

Carole disappeared between two friends, and soon there was only Mrs. Boyden and Scotty left in the classroom.

Scotty ignored the giggles coming from the hallway. Mrs. Boyden looked up from her gray metal desk. Still holding his elbow, Scotty said, "three-oh-one."

"Very good," Mrs. Boyden said.

That weekend, Scotty repeatedly grabbed the Judge's wrist with both hands. He studied the Judge's watch. Scotty's face contorted as he did his figuring.

"Seven . . . twenty," Scotty said.

"Correct."

Scotty smiled.

Two minutes later he grabbed the Judge's wrist again.

"Seven . . . twenty."

"Close enough," the Judge said.

"Seven-twenty-two to be exact," Maggie said, looking at her Minnie Mouse watch.

"Close enough," Scotty shouted back.

Throughout that evening and for the next several days, Scotty barked out times.

"Evidence," the Judge liked to say, "that you're learning things, Scotty."

"Yeah," Scotty would say. "Evidence."

"And why do we gather evidence?"

"To make our case."

"Yes. And why do we want to make a case?"

"To prove we're right."

"Correct, Scotty." The Judge extended his stocking feet. "Will you rub them?"

Scotty pulled off the socks. The Judge's feet were dry with white, flaky patches—a remnant from his World War II tour of duty.

"It's nice of you to do this for your old man."

Did Scotty have a choice?

"Ugly feet, aren't they?" the Judge liked to brag. "Do you know why they're ugly?"

Scotty shook his head, even though he knew why. Scotty began to massage the Judge's feet. Then the Judge leaned back and closed his eyes.

"It's a reminder—evidence—that I served my country. Some people lost arms and legs; sometimes they even gave their lives. I was lucky. To go to war and only have to give up my handsome feet."

"Your feet sure are ugly," Scotty said, stopping the massage. He shook out his hands.

"You're not stopping, are you?"

"I'm tired."

"More." The Judge wiggled his toes.

"But . . ."

"More."

And Scotty continued to rub.

"Good boy."

Yes.

And then, as the family watched *My Three Sons,* the phone rang. Scotty leapt to his feet and scrambled down the hallway. He stood on one of the kitchen chairs to answer the phone.

"Ocean residence, Scotty spea—"

A similar high-pitched voice interrupted. "Hey!" the excited, out-of-breath voice exclaimed. "It's my dad!"

Scotty recognized Tom Conway's voice.

"He's coming home."

(7)

The morning of Sergeant Conway's return, the Judge sent
Scotty out to retrieve the newspaper.

Outside, Scotty saw a figure moving in the Conways' front
yard. He stood watching until the Judge impatiently swung
open the screen door and said, "Scotty." But Scotty pointed
down the street to Mrs. Conway, who wandered about their
front yard in her white nightgown. The Judge pulled on his
slacks and walked with Scotty down the street. The streetlights
were still on and the sun would be rising soon. They moved
close enough to see that Liz Conway was emptying jars full of
change into her front yard, spreading the coins the way a farmer
would feed pigs.

The Judge whispered to Scotty, "Now why do you think
she'd do that?"

Scotty shrugged.

Liz Conway saw the Ocean men standing across the street.
"I've been saving since he left," she said. "Saving these last two
years."

The Judge had always thought of Liz Conway as a simple-
minded wife of a career soldier, but as he watched her, he
began to rethink what he had held to be true.

"Scotty," the Judge said, "I want you to stay off their
property."

"Why would she throw out all that money?" Scotty asked the Judge.

"I don't know, Scotty," the Judge said, even though he had a pretty good idea why.

Scotty wore only underwear as he watched the morning cartoons. He sat with his hand on the channel knob. He flipped from show to show—*Heckle and Jeckle* (the know-it-all magpies), *Scooby-Doo,* and *H. R. Pufnstuf*—until the doorbell interrupted him.

He found Tom Conway standing on the Oceans' porch, smiling big. Scotty had hardly opened the door when Tom spouted, "Our yard's off-limits. That's what my mom says. She's got a surprise planned."

Tom's father was a sergeant in Vietnam and he rode in tanks. In honor of his return, Tom dressed in the same pretend army uniform he wore on Halloween, minus the bloody headband.

Scotty asked Tom if he wanted to come inside to watch cartoons.

Tom said, "No—a soldier has to be ready at all times."

So Scotty put on pants and a T-shirt and they stood around the Ocean front yard.

"The men get to wear uniforms."

"Yeah," Scotty said.

At the Conway house, the phone kept ringing and Liz Conway scurried around getting her daughter Donna ready. The Conway women were wearing identical dresses, which Liz had made out of the same flowered fabric. She started sewing when she got word that Sergeant Conway was coming home, sewing round the clock to finish them in time.

"She's got some kind of special surprise," Tom said. "My mom's been smiling all morning." Tom bent down to tie Scotty's tennis shoe.

Standing at the base of the Conway driveway, Liz shouted, "Tom!"

The boys turned and saw Liz Conway. With a large pink bow in her hair and wearing the flowered dress, she looked gift-wrapped.

"Tom, time to go!"

Tom sprinted home.

Scotty waited in the yard and watched them drive away. Then he sat under the big sycamore tree, and even though it was forbidden, he pried bark off the tree trunk with his fingers. As he broke it into small pieces, he thought how nice it would be to be covered in bark.

Back in the house, he flipped channels. Cartoons were over. It was either *Wide World of Sports* or college football or an old movie on Channel 5.

Maggie fixed herself a bowl of ice cream and watched from the sofa. At a commercial break, she went to the bathroom and Scotty moved closer to the TV. He couldn't believe what he was seeing.

He stared at the TV, studying every move, memorizing every detail: her blue-and-white-striped shirt, her shoulder-length hair pulled back with a red bandanna. She sailed with a man, in a white boat with a light brown deck—the trees were bright green and the water an unbelievable blue. As a Glenn Campbell-like voice sang about Salem and springtime, the wind blew the boat and the couple floated around the large lake. So much can happen in thirty seconds. The television showed this woman slowly bring a lit cigarette to her mouth—done as if there were nothing better on this earth. When the cigarette touched her lips, she inhaled—the camera cut away before she exhaled, so Scotty exhaled for her.

"Does Scotty have a girlfriend?" Maggie said from the hall-way.

"No," Scotty snapped.

"Does too."

Maggie pushed Scotty out of the way. "My turn," she announced. "You've hogged the TV all day."

Scotty, stunned, moved away from the TV as Maggie turned it to *American Bandstand*. Dick Clark was announcing the musical guests for the week.

"Claire," Maggie shouted, "Peaches and Herb! The 1910 Fruitgum Company!"

Scotty knew he was outnumbered. He was climbing the stairs as Claire rushed by him screaming as if at an actual concert.

The Oceans' second television, a black-and-white model with old-fashioned rabbit ears (a gift at the Judge and Joan's wedding in 1953) sat on its own portable stand in the master bedroom.

When he reached the top of the stairs, Scotty pushed open the Judge's door.

"Don't you know how to knock?" the Judge snapped. He had been napping in his clothes, lying on top of the covers of his bed.

Scotty quickly pulled the door closed and went to his room. He didn't know what to do. He lay on his unmade bed. He looked out his bedroom window. He could see over the fence into the Crows' backyard. Two construction workers sat in the grass enjoying their lunches, which they took from their all-black construction worker lunch pails. The workers had dug out a big square patch of dirt. Near them was a portable cement mixer and two unopened bags of cement. Tom Conway had told Scotty that he'd heard the new neighbor was getting a basketball court of his own.

Scotty picked up his pink and blue clay piggy bank. He'd lost the black rubber circular stopper that was to keep the coins in place. His bank was empty, but he shook it anyway, in case a coin had gotten trapped in one of the pig's ceramic legs. But there was nothing inside, only air.

Then Scotty found the plastic bag that held the pieces to his checker set. He dumped them out on the floor and stacked them, one on top of the other, until they began to lean. He knocked over the checkers and listened to see if anyone was heading toward his room concerned about the noise.

Downstairs his sisters were perfecting their dance moves to "Incense and Peppermints." He had seen their routine too many times. They jumped up and down on the sofa, shrieking—anyway Scotty knew he was the better dancer.

In his sock drawer, Scotty found his Silly Putty. He removed it from its red plastic egg. Pulling it slowly, he stretched it long, as if it were taffy. It could go forever, he thought. Then, rolling it between the palms of his hands, he made it into a ball and headed to the bathroom where he bounced it on the linoleum. It bounced back into his hands.

Scotty felt like taking a bite. Its pinkish, flesh-toned color tempted him. Perhaps its taste would be a blend of bubble gum and cookie dough. But Scotty remembered the third grader named Doug Clary who'd swallowed a chunk of Silly Putty the previous year. An ambulance was called, and a doctorlike person had stuck a tube down Doug Clary's throat and pumped his stomach.

So Scotty never tasted the Silly Putty: He knew to look to others who had preceded him—a history of mistakes had been made by other boys and girls, fourth and fifth graders now. They were examples, *evidence* of what could happen if . . .

Chad Linn went backward down the fourth grade slide and cracked his head and Alicia Albright went to sleep with bubble gum in her mouth, woke up with the wad of gum wedged in her hair, and had to have part of her head shaved. Scotty knew not to do those things.

Mary Beth Swift's brother Donny had tried to hang on to the window of a moving school bus, but he fell under the wheel and his head was squashed. *Don't hang on bus windows* was a clear lesson. Scotty thought of Donny Swift, in fact all children thought of Donny Swift, whenever they drank from the water fountain at Clover Hills Elementary School. A small plaque had been hung above the water fountain in Donny's memory. And with each sip of water, all children were reminded not to hang on the windows of moving school buses, and to remember as they drank from the fountain that life is precious, cool, and refreshing like the water shooting at them. Be thirsty for life. That is what they were told.

Sometimes Scotty liked to pull at the Silly Putty—when he did that, it would break like a biscuit. But his favorite Silly Putty activity was to mash it flat, pancakelike (inevitably he'd think of the bus squashing Donny Swift's head). Then he'd press the Putty over a comic in the newspaper, push down, then peel it off. And on the Silly Putty would be the words or the image. The Sunday comics were best to use, as they were printed in color.

It was during these alone times, when doing his favorite activities—squashing ants, picking at tree bark, or placing Silly Putty over the *Family Circus* or *Peanuts*—that Scotty had little pictorial flashes, hintlike flirtations that his mother was coming home.

He didn't know why he knew this but he went downstairs and shouted to his dancing sisters, "Mom's coming, I think!" When they didn't answer, he ran out to the curb where he sat the rest of the afternoon, waiting for the yellow of her car to appear at the end of the street. And, he decided, when he saw her car, he'd run toward it, and when she stopped in the middle of the street, he'd climb into the passenger side, reach over the stick shift, and cling to her as they drove on.

But later it was the Conways' Ford Falcon station wagon that started up the street. Scotty watched from behind the telephone pole nearest his house. Mrs. Conway put the car in park, turned off the ignition. The car doors swung open. Tom was the first one out. His sister followed. The sergeant stood looking at his house, his freshly mowed yard, his property. Tom stood next to him in identical dress except that while the sergeant wore military boots, Tom wore Keds. The sergeant took a drag from his cigarette and looked at his wife. Scotty thought, Where are those cigarette people? This would make a great commercial.

Mrs. Conway held close to her husband and the family went inside.

Scotty went into his house. He turned on the TV to watch whatever he could find; maybe his Salem girl would return. Within minutes, though, he heard shrieks of laughter coming from outside. He pressed his face to the picture window. He saw movement in the Conways' front yard. Outside he stood by the Ocean mailbox to get a better view.

Tom Conway and his sister were running around their yard, bending over, giggling, whooping, hollering.

Scotty walked nonchalantly to the Conways' house where he balanced like a circus performer on the curb. While he did this, he watched Tom and his sister fill their containers. Tom had a coffee can with string for a handle; his sister Donna carried a big peanut butter jar. They gathered the change. *Clink* and *clunk* filled the air. Tom was on his knees, moving about fast. Everywhere Scotty looked, he saw coins in the grass.

"You want help?" Scotty asked.

"No."

"You don't have to share it. I'll help you."

"No!"

"Course you could pay me *but you don't have to* . . ."

"Get off of our property."

"But . . ."

"GET OFF OUR PROPERTY!"

Looking at the Conway house, Scotty saw in an upstairs window Sergeant and Mrs. Conway kissing. The kiss looked desperate, somewhat sloppy. Sergeant Conway removed his uniform top and lifted off his T-shirt. When Mrs. Conway looked out the window to check on her kids, she saw Scotty staring up at her. The sergeant put his arms around her stomach. His hands cupped her breasts; she giggled and slowly lowered the shade.

Scotty looked at the Conway kids. They were rich.

(8)

The phone rang. Scotty wasn't the one closest to the receiver. That didn't prevent him from trying to get to it first. He crawled under the kitchen table, pushed aside a chair, and was starting to stand when the Judge reached over effortlessly, saying, "I've got it."

If Scotty had answered it, this is what he would have heard: the sound of a woman choking, struggling to speak.

"Hello?" said the Judge.

On the other end of the phone, the choking continued. Spurts of heavy breathing. Then silence.

"Hello?" repeated the Judge.

Aware that Scotty was waiting at his feet, the Judge tried to remain calm. "Yes," the Judge pretended. "I'm glad you called."

Scotty liked being on the kitchen floor. He liked being under the kitchen table and waiting for legs to come walking past.

"Scotty, run along."

Scotty pulled open the drawer below the silverware drawer, the drawer full of tins of shoe polish, brushes, and buffers. Under the kitchen table, he began to polish the Judge's shoes.

"No, Scotty."

"But . . ."

"You can polish them later. Run along!"

Scotty crawled out from under the table, across the kitchen floor, and disappeared into the dining room.

The Judge returned to the phone.

"Joan?" he whispered. "Are you all right?"

The choking had a gurgle sound to it.

"Where are you?"

Scotty continued his crawl through the living room, passing in front of Maggie and Claire, who watched *Room 222*.

"Don't block the TV!"

Scotty kept on—he turned right and headed back to the kitchen.

"Tell me where you are."

But the gurgling stopped and the phone line went click and the dial tone purred.

Scotty crawled past the Judge, disappearing again into the dining room, crossing the living room, back down the hall, past the Judge, who now sat numbly, unaware of his giggling boy.

Late that night the Judge was awakened by a second call. Joan's father telephoned the Judge to inform him that Joan had almost choked to death on her own vomit. She had agreed to go to a hospital in Minnesota that would help her. Her father would be driving her that morning. "We just thought you should know."

The Judge thanked him for the call. He turned on the lamp above his headboard and wrote down the address where the children could write.

"She'd like to hear from them, I'm sure," Joan's father said.

The Judge was so eager to tell his children that he woke Claire with the good news. She was pleased and hugged her father. Maggie said, "That's good" and turned over and fell back asleep. Then the Judge entered Scotty's room where he stood over the bed. Scotty's face looked sweet and peaceful but his body lay, pretzel-like, pulled in every direction—it looked as if his son had been dropped from thirty stories. He wondered how a boy could sleep in such a mangled shape.

He touched him lightly on the forehead, stroking his bangs to the side. Then he tapped lightly on an exposed shoulder.

Scotty's eyes cracked open, then closed quickly. The Judge

got on his knees and wrapped his arms around Scotty. He hadn't shaved and his beard stubble felt like little knives.

"Ow! It hurts . . ."

The Judge let go. He didn't do this well.

Scotty pulled the covers over his head, curled into a ball, and said, "Go away."

The Judge laughed at Scotty.

"Not funny," Scotty called out from under the sheet.

But the Judge kept laughing.

"It's not funny," Scotty repeated. He waited under the sheet, wetness where his mouth was, the features of his face jutting out, his nose, his chin and forehead defined by the taut sheet.

Scotty felt the mattress sink as the Judge sat on the edge of his bed. Then he heard a low groaning sound. His father sounded like an animal on a TV special—a bear, perhaps, eating another, smaller animal. Scotty squeezed his eyes shut as his father gasped for air. Finally, when Scotty lowered the sheet, he saw the Judge's face, hit with broken rays of the morning sun, drenched with tears, his chest and neck shivering.

The mattress on Scotty's bed sank lower as the Judge let his legs release, all of his weight on the bed. The loud creaking from the added weight made Scotty think the support boards underneath were about to snap. The Judge covered his face with his hands and Scotty waited for him to stop.

(9)

"Class," Mrs. Boyden said, "this is Tim Myerly. He moved here from Ohio. This is his first day."

Tim Myerly had to sit on Mrs. Boyden's stool until Mr. Fry, the janitor, brought in an extra desk.

"We have four rows of six desks. One row will need to move back. One row will have to have seven desks."

"Yippee," Scotty said.

A soft knock came on the door and Mrs. Boyden opened it. Scotty caught a glimpse of a woman's arm holding a lunch pail.

"My boy forgot this," the woman said.

Mrs. Boyden took the lunch pail from the woman, thanked her, and closed the door.

"Tim," Mrs. Boyden said, holding up the yellow lunch pail shaped like a doghouse. Written in bright red letters was the word "Snoopy."

Dan Burkhett snickered and Scotty said, "What a stupid. His mother brought his lunch."

The boys near Scotty laughed (all of them had mothers at home). Scotty was laughing, too, when he saw the new boy's mom pass by the classroom window. She waved to her boy. Tim Myerly's mom was a small woman with an eager gait and a sweetness that most boys would take for granted. Scotty watched as she walked past and he stayed staring after she was gone.

It hadn't taken long for the mothers of Scotty's friends and classmates to hear that Joan Ocean had been hospitalized. They began to jockey gently for Scotty's approval. Not that they wanted to raise the boy, but collectively they wanted him to know that all mothers didn't disappear; all mothers didn't end up in the hospital.

Shari Tussey's mom had straight yellow hair and she always smiled when she spoke. Even when she yelled, she smiled— her lips pulled back revealing her large teeth. She looks like a beaver, Scotty thought. No mother should look like a beaver.

Ruth Rethman's mother brought a treat to class one Friday in November: Saltine crackers with honey from real bees. Ruth Rethman's mother pointed out the honeycomb in the honey jar. She seemed much too nice, trying to win the friendship of Ruth's classmates. Bribery. She couldn't win Scotty's love.

Craig Hunt's mom had cold hands and loved to hug Craig's friends. Craig loved insects and Estes rockets and, most of all, his mom, who parceled out his Halloween candy, a piece a day, which each year lasted well into May. No mother holds on to candy.

And there were more mothers. Nice mothers and pretty mothers, and sometimes a mother would be nice and pretty both. Bev Fowler had such a mom. Bev and her mother wore identical glasses. Black frames, almost square, thick lenses. Whenever Scotty saw Bev Fowler and her mother, he stared extensively at the glasses. The lenses were thick like pond ice. You could skate over her eyes, Scotty thought. Bev's eyes doubled in size if somebody got close enough. Bev Fowler's mom accompanied the class on a field trip to the Iowa Historical Society to look at authentic American Indian arrowheads and clothing. Scotty spent most of his time staring at Bev Fowler's mom. She kept touching her daughter's hair, stroking it lightly. They looked like they shared secrets, Bev and her mom, and Scotty could identify. His mother always stroked his hair when they shared their secrets.

And there were never-before-seen mothers and new-to-town mothers. Scotty had just seen such a mom: Tim Myerly's.

(10)

Scotty listened as his neighbor Andrew Crow explained. "This is junior high information, Ocean. Do you know that?" Scotty squinted, as if squinting would help him hear. He couldn't believe his luck. Only minutes earlier he'd heard the bouncing of Andrew Crow's basketball. Scotty tried to walk across his yard quietly but the crunching of the orange and yellow leaves below him gave him away. And when he reached the edge of his yard, he noticed Andrew Crow looking over at him, a Spalding basketball held with two hands, as if he were Atlas holding the world. "Come on over," Andrew said. Other than his pant leg catching on the top of the fence, Scotty climbed over in his usual manner. He fell to the ground but stood up quickly and brushed his shirt and pants and smiled, but Andrew Crow had gone back to shooting baskets. Scotty moved to the edge of the court. Andrew dribbled between his legs, tried a hook shot but missed the basket completely. Scotty thought he better make himself useful, and chased after the ball. Andrew Crow held out his hands, as if to say "Throw it to me." Scotty bounced the ball to Andrew Crow. Scotty had found his purpose.

In all the time they had been neighbors, Andrew Crow hadn't said much. But now he was talking, and Scotty listened close, because he wanted to soak up every word.

"Junior high information is what I'm giving you. Are you listening?"

Scotty nodded.

"Are you!"

"Yes."

Andrew Crow dribbled the basketball, then stopped. He looked directly into Scotty's eyes.

"First base you kiss."

"Okay."

"Have you kissed anybody?"

Scotty quickly replayed his kissing memories. "Carole Staley kissed me. Right here," he said, pointing to his elbow.

"Gotta be on the lips, Ocean, for it to be first base."

"Oh." Scotty remembered kissing his mother repeatedly and his sisters, too. "My mom and sisters—"

"Mothers and sisters don't count."

"Okay."

"Now if I were to kiss one of your sisters . . . let's say Claire . . . if I were to kiss *Claire,* it would be first base. But if you were to kiss—"

"It wouldn't count."

"Right." Andrew dribbled the basketball twice, drove toward the hoop, and missed a lay-up. Scotty followed after the ball, which had bounced off the court into a mound of raked leaves. He brought it back.

Taking the ball, Andrew continued. "Second base you put your hands on her boobs."

Scotty didn't know whether to cover his ears or what.

"You better hope she has boobs. Your sister Maggie has no boobs—if I put my hands there, they'd be like big pimples. That'd be no fun."

Scotty nodded in agreement, as if he understood, as if he knew from experience. Andrew tossed the ball from a great distance, missing the basket completely. Scotty retrieved the ball.

"Third base is a finger. Maybe two fingers if she's over fifteen."

Scotty looked puzzled. He thought, a finger? Scotty had seen a magician at Jimmy Lamson's birthday party do an amazing trick. He raised a hatchet above his head suddenly, brought it down quickly, then held up a bloody finger, severed. Later, because one of the kids watching started screaming, the magician revealed the finger to be rubber. The blood turned out to be red paint. Scotty got to hold the finger. How realistic, he thought at the time. How lifelike. Weeks later he came across a box of those fingers in the novelty section at Kmart.

Scotty's face betrayed his confusion now. Why should it be a third base when a guy can go to the mall and buy a finger? Or a whole box of fingers?

Sensing Scotty's confusion, Andrew stopped dribbling and elaborated. "A guy uses a finger—one from his own hand—to penetrate the girl."

Penetrate, Scotty thought. Penetrate must be a sixth grade word, a junior high word.

"Stick in, enter, pierce—like that."

"Oh," Scotty said.

"Between her legs is a hole. It goes by many names." Andrew listed several.

Later, Scotty could only remember one name. Vagina. It sounded eternal, vagina, like a vacation land.

At dinner that night he studied his sisters. Each of them must have a hole. Had any of them been fingered? Before dessert Scotty asked Claire the meaning of a word he struggled to pronounce. She replied, "The word is penetrate." She said the word, spelled it, used it in a sentence, then said it again.

The Judge said, "Correct."

Scotty thought about the word "vagina." It was a word he did not need defined. But he wished he could spell it. If only he could, Scotty thought, then he would write it a million times in a row or until his hand fell off, whichever came first.

(II)

Scotty sprinted for the phone, which he answered in mid-ring.

"Hello, young man!" a male voice said. This is a happy man I'm talking to, Scotty thought.

"Hi!" said Scotty, sending back a happy sound.

"What are you doing tonight?"

"Nothing."

"Well, young man, is the lady of the house there?"

Scotty went, "Uhm."

"May I speak with your mother?"

"No."

"Is there a time I could call back?"

"She's not here."

"When might she be returning?"

Scotty said nothing. There was nothing to say.

He hung up the phone, walked across the kitchen to look at the brochure that the Judge had taped on the refrigerator. St. Mary's Retreat in Rochester, Minnesota.

"Looks like a church," Scotty said once.

"It's not a church, though," the Judge said. "It's a place where people go to get well."

Scotty would decorate the letters Claire and Maggie wrote. Sometimes he drew in the margins or colored around words.

Mostly he'd print his name all over each piece of paper: "Scotty," as if it were an advertisement. "Scotty," as if he were campaigning. "Scotty."

Joan wrote postcards back in which she always thanked her kids for keeping her mailbox filled. "Send me your drawings and watercolors, *please*. Make me a masterpiece. My walls are too, too bare."

(12)

For days Scotty only thought about his conversation with Andrew Crow.

Fourth base, the home run, had no appeal, Scotty decided. It didn't make sense to him. He didn't see how it was possible. Anyway he felt more comfortable with his fingers. He used them daily, moved them every which way, and, of course, he was adept at hand shadows.

A week after his conversation with Andrew Crow, and after the class had watched a short film on Johnny Appleseed, Mrs. Boyden asked Scotty if he'd like to demonstrate his talent for making shadows. "I've heard so much about it," Mrs. Boyden said. "Now seems like a good time."

Suddenly Scotty was making his way down the aisle, and his classmates were whispering, "Make the bird, make the rabbit, make the alligator!"

Mrs. Boyden left the projector light on for Scotty. She looked forward to watching him, of course, but she encouraged him for a more important reason. Early in her career, Mrs. Boyden had taught a young girl who loved to announce her assessment of the weather. This girl did so every morning after the Pledge of Allegiance. This girl grew up to be a weather-woman for a station in Chicago. Mrs. Boyden felt somehow she had done her part to nurture. She wondered if the same might hold true for Scotty Ocean; perhaps he would grow up to be a puppeteer and one day work on the *Kukla, Fran, and Ollie* show.

One could never know.

Scotty approached the center of the room. He stuck one hand in front of the projector light. It looked huge on the screen. He made a fist. The class grew quiet. Mrs. Boyden leaned on the windowsill, ready, too, to enjoy the show. Most classmates called out for the bird, a few requested the shark, and Carole Staley begged for the butterfly. Carole Staley's mother had told Carole, who told Scotty that she (Carole) had been, in a previous incarnation, a butterfly. Carole suggested perhaps she and Scotty had maybe been butterflies together. Scotty could think of no worse punishment than being the same creature as Carole Staley.

He held his fist motionless for a long time. The requests for various animals came pouring in. Finally, Mrs. Boyden quieted the group. "Scotty won't do his show until everyone is quiet. Isn't that right, Scotty?"

"Yes, ma'am."

When all was quiet, except for the hum of the movie projector, Scotty began. "This is a new bird I've been working on," he said. "The first time ever seen."

"Ooo," whispered some classmates. Mrs. Boyden beamed.

Scotty extended one finger, his forefinger, and wiggled it slowly. "This is a special kind of bird," he announced. "The third base bird!"

Only David Bumgartner and Dan Burkhett laughed. Only Bumgartner and Burkhett knew the meaning of third base and only because Scotty had told them. Mrs. Boyden apparently knew the meaning, too, because she promptly turned off the projector and sent the others off to an early recess. She then informed Scotty he would be staying inside.

The worst punishment.

As the others played outdoors—skipping rope, swinging, going down the slide and up the rope ladder—Scotty sat at his desk.

Mrs. Boyden crossed her flabby arms and stared at Scotty. Then she took out a sheet of paper. "I'm going to write your father a note. What do you think I should say?"

"Nothing."

"Nothing? I think I have to tell him something."

"No! Please!"

Scotty imagined the Judge's reaction: big hairy fists coming down hard on the kitchen table, the Judge's voice, low and absolute, yelling so loud it hurt his ears, and Scotty undoing his belt and lowering his pants and feeling the slap of those hands, the sting from the Judge's wedding ring, and so Scotty begged Mrs. Boyden, "Please, don't write a note."

Mrs. Boyden stopped. Scotty was about to burst. So she put away her paper. "Where would a boy like you learn about such things?"

Scotty shrugged.

"Who taught you such an awful gesture?"

Scotty stared at his desk.

"Not your father, not your sisters."

"No."

Mrs. Boyden told him to approach her desk. She handed Scotty a blank sheet of paper. He returned to his desk where he used a green Husky pencil to write "I am sorry" over and over.

After the other kids returned from recess, it was the time of day when all her students put their heads down on their desks, and Mrs. Boyden would read a story.

"Today's story is one of my favorites. 'Mike Mulligan and His Steam Shovel.' It's the story of a steam shovel that digs himself into a very deep hole."

Mrs. Boyden began to read. Glancing up at the class, she noticed that Scotty was still hunched over the piece of paper, writing "I am sorry." Mrs. Boyden stopped reading and said, "That's enough, Scotty."

But Scotty continued anyway. He was in the middle of printing his thirty-seventh "sorry" when the sheet of paper was taken away.

Scotty looked up at his teacher.

"That's enough," she said with a smile. She returned to her stool and continued reading.

After school, Mrs. Boyden worked on her lesson plan for the following day. Before going home, she put her desk in order. She crossed to the windows to close the blinds. These were her end-of-the-day rituals, and they gave her a sense of completion. Passing by the desks of her students, she often saw remnants of the day: a scrap of paper, a broken crayon, some indication that minutes earlier little boys and girls had been learning.

When Mrs. Boyden came to Scotty's desk in the middle of the classroom, she suddenly stopped. In all her years of teaching, she'd never seen anything like it. "I am sorry" was printed countless times in pencil across the surface of Scotty's desk. So many "I am sorry's" that it was obvious to her that Scotty had gotten the point, so many that Mrs. Boyden began to feel ill. So she took a bucket from under the classroom sink, filled it with warm, sudsy water—she wet a sponge and scrubbed Scotty's desk clean.

(13)

Sometimes at night when he bathed, Scotty felt a vague memory, blurry, but it hung in his thoughts. Whenever he bathed, he concentrated hard to fight through its fuzziness. He remembered sitting in warm water at one end. Across from him, covered in bubbles, two brown nipples and a clump of hair between her legs, his mother. She'd hand him soap. He washed, or so he thought, he didn't know. Only the breasts, her hair, and the space in between her legs held any clarity.

Don't get fuzzy, he thought.

Scotty's baths kept getting longer. He scrubbed and scrubbed, washing himself repeatedly, so that when Joan returned, she'd find him clean, smelling nice, no dirt under his nails. And the longer he stayed in the tub, he thought, the better he could remember her.

(14)

It was a Saturday afternoon in November when Tom Conway showed Scotty Ocean his father's hidden treasure.

His parents' closet had been padlocked but not with precision. Tom had figured out how to get the closet door opened, and he allowed Scotty a glimpse. Hanging from the wall were machine guns, bayonet blades—a cache of weapons.

"Authentic," Tom Conway said.

Scotty reached to touch the muzzle of an M-16 rifle. In drawers were pistols and knives. In a shoebox, wrapped like Christmas ornaments, were two hand grenades.

"You pull the plug—then you toss."

Scotty said, "Can I touch one?"

Tom said, "For a buck."

Scotty paid him later in nickels and dimes. He held the grenade. He felt its ridges. It was heavy. Heavy like a bowling ball but the size of a baseball.

"So you pull this?"

"Yep."

Scotty imagined yanking out the metal pin.

"But don't."

"I won't."

"You only got seconds after you pull the pin."

"Guys in movies use their mouth."

"I know, Ocean."

"Ow." Scotty imagined his teeth biting into a grenade. He wondered if his teeth would snap. "Ow," he said again.

"Quit going 'ow.' "

"What if you pulled the pin and forgot to throw it—or didn't throw it in time?"

"It'd blow off your hand, your face."

"You'd die?"

"Maybe. You'd get metal chunks under your skin. You'd wish you were dead."

(15)

The week before Thanksgiving, Brian Eldridge had his eighth birthday party. His three best friends slept over and then other boys including Scotty arrived for cake and games.

Claire remarked that Brian Eldridge just wanted more presents. "And the more guests, the more presents, am I right?"

"Yeah," Scotty said. Of course Claire was right.

Brian had been given an Art-a-Matic. A red plastic boxlike container with an electric motor that spun five-by-seven-inch white cards. Plastic bottles of the three primary colors and a fourth bottle of white could be dribbled or squirted onto the spinning page. Centrifugal force sent the paint splattering outward.

Heads bumped as the boys pushed for position. Only a few could watch from above at a time. And it astonished them, the way something blank could become colorful, like the fireworks on *The Wonderful World of Disney,* and so easy, just drops of paint.

Scotty tried to ignore the Art-a-Matic's popularity. His gift, a Butterfly yo-yo, which Claire helped him pick out at Wirtz's drugstore, wasn't the hit that he'd hoped it would be. It remained in its packaging next to Brian's other unpopular gifts— a Slinky Caterpillar and a Wham-O glow-in-the-dark Frisbee.

Brian's cake was chocolate and Scotty hated chocolate cake, but he did like the punch, orange Hi-C mixed with 7-UP, so he stayed mainly around the punch bowl, where over the course of the afternoon, a large, doughnut-shaped ice cube floated, then melted.

Brian's mother unwrapped a package of prematted frames.

Each party guest would get to take home their own memento of the day.

Fortunately, before the other boys could put pressure on Scotty to take his turn, the paint supply began to run out.

Brian's mother told Scotty the next time he came over he'd get his chance at spin art. She wrapped up a piece of cake in Saran Wrap and said, "How about some extra?"

The three boys who spent the night—Richard Hibbs, Chip Fisher, and Craig Hunt—bragged about their night.

"We didn't sleep," Brian claimed. "Told ghost stories."

Scotty didn't spend nights away from home. He had no interest. If his mother returned and he wasn't home, she might worry about him. And if she were to come back, Scotty didn't want to miss a thing.

Craig Hunt approached Scotty and held out his still-wet Art-a-Matic spin painting.

Scotty didn't know what to do or say.

Then Craig mentioned how he'd seen an even bigger Art-a-Matic at the Iowa State Fair. He told Scotty how if you brought your own T-shirt and paid a dollar, you could make a painting on your own shirt. Proudly holding up his spin painting, Craig said, "Good, huh?"

"No," Scotty said.

"Say it's good."

Craig Hunt had been held back because he was thickheaded and a behavior problem. He was by far the biggest kid in Mrs. Boyden's second grade class, and he was already eight, eight from the first day. In fact, with Craig's birthday coming up in March, he'd be the first to turn nine.

Sticking his painting into Scotty's face, Craig Hunt said, "Tell me it's good."

Scotty remembered that the week before, Craig Hunt had dropped a fourth grade boy during recess with a swift, effortless kick to the boy's groin. The boy fell over shrieking in pain. Tom Conway claimed to have seen it happen. By the next recess other boys had been told and soon the whole school seemed to know. Avoid Craig Hunt whenever possible. And if he traps you or you sit next to him on the bus, be nice and agreeable.

Scotty imagined the pointed toe of Craig Hunt's cowboy boot landing between his legs. He didn't want to scream or turn blue in the face.

Which is why Scotty Ocean agreed that Craig Hunt's spin art was actual art.

At show-and-tell later that week, Christine Bettis displayed three pages of Spirograph drawings. Intricate patterns of geometric designs, symmetrical swirls made in red, blue, black, and green ink. All you do is hold the pen, Scotty thought.

Scotty remembered Joan complaining about Spirograph. "Anyone can do that," she had told her children. "It takes no skill." Etch-A-Sketch, Lite-Brite, and an automatic pencil with a goofy, beelike face called the Bizzy Buzz Buzz Drawing Set— these were cheating toys.

And the previous Christmas, when Maggie asked for the Barbie drawing kit, which, through tracing, enabled a person to draw the newest teen fashions, Joan said a resolute no. A crying Maggie said, "But I want to make art, too." Joan explained that anything that only required tracing is not art. "Anyone can trace!"

"Be originals," Joan had tried to engrain in them. "All you

need is blank paper and something to draw with. A pen, a pencil, your own blood."

Scotty understood the pen and pencil. But blood? What was he supposed to do, he wondered—cut himself, prick his finger? Claire explained that what Joan meant was that they were to paint from their heart. The heart pumps blood, she went on. But Scotty thought Claire was wrong, and he hoped that the next time he scraped a knee or had a bloody nose he'd have a sheet of blank paper nearby, for he'd let the blood drip and then quickly use his fingers to make a drawing of himself or a house with a yard or maybe something abstract, which he knew Joan would like.

(16)

Mrs. Boyden announced to the class that she had a special treat. Then she introduced the artist Miss Clarissa Jude to the class. "It's an honor," Mrs. Boyden said, "to have an *actual* artist come to our classroom. Aren't we lucky, class?"

"Yes, Mrs. Boyden," the children said.

Miss Jude was the most popular artist in the greater Des Moines area. A painter of still lifes, she specialized in bowls of fruit.

Standing in front of the class, with gray hair, pinched lips and brittle, blotched hands, Miss Jude spoke to the students about art. Her nasal voice irritated Scotty. He wanted a teacher with pizzazz. He wanted an artist like his mother, a smiling artist with pretty eyes and long hair and soft hands.

As Miss Jude spoke, the door swung open suddenly. Joan Ocean stood in the doorway, her paint shirt specked with every color, a large brush in her hand. She dipped the brush in her mouth and painted a mustache on Miss Jude; then she painted flowers coming out Miss Jude's ears . . .

"That's enough, Scotty!" Mrs. Boyden called out to Scotty, who was laughing so hard he'd covered his face. "That's enough!"

When Scotty looked up, he saw the eyes of his classmates staring at him. He saw Mrs. Boyden poised ready to come down the aisle after him. He saw Miss Jude standing by the blackboard, a fake smile on her face. Miss Jude had no mustache, no flowers out her ears, and for Scotty, his mother was nowhere to be seen.

Miss Jude resumed her talk about art. She told the class they could paint whatever they wanted. "Just so it's real," she said.

When she asked what the budding artists might have in mind for subjects, hands rose in the air. "A dinosaur," said one. "A tree." "A swing set!"

"Those are all real things," Miss Jude said.

Yeah, but not as real as what I'm going to paint, Scotty thought.

Carole Staley and Scotty Ocean sat next to each other every time there was Art. Carole's crush on Scotty was no longer a secret. Ever since she kissed his forearm, everybody had known. Scotty detested Carole and avoided her at all times. But during Art in Mrs. Boyden's class, he gravitated toward her, often sitting with her at the same table, sharing crayons, construction paper, and finger paints. It was during Art that Carole's kissing missions ceased, and Scotty left her pigtails alone.

Only Art could call a truce.

And with the arrival of Miss Clarissa Jude, for an afternoon, they would be inseparable, taking over the table in the back of the room. Sitting as far away as possible, they spread out large sheets of white paper. They moved quickly up to the front of the room to secure the best paints. Carole carried as many plastic paint bottles as she could. Scotty followed with only two.

"I'm just using black and white today," he said.

He watched as Carole took red and green, mixed them, squirted in some yellow, used a big thick brush to stir, dropped in three dribbles of blue. She painted a sun in the corner of the page. She mixed more colors. "Purple comes from red and blue," she said, looking over at Scotty who stared at his paper. "Scotty, what are you painting?"

"Oh, only the realest thing I know."

All morning they worked, forgetting about the time, not even hearing the announcement over the intercom about the next day's Thanksgiving assembly. And when the kids were excused for lunch, Scotty and Carole kept on painting.

"Okay, you two. Finish up. You've got to eat. Artists have to eat."

When they returned from lunch, the paintings had been hung across the chalkboard, and along the bank of windows.

"Twenty-five paintings, boys and girls, and Miss Jude has stayed here to judge your work. She will give it a critique. Let's thank Miss Jude."

The kids clapped.

Carole's painting hung third from the left. Scotty's had been pinned on the far end. He knew from the placement of his painting that he would go last. He loved being last.

Miss Jude started with Lucy Titman's painting.

"Hmmm, very nice, Lucy. Very nice. Can everyone see that it's an apple?"

"Yes," the kids said.

"Can you see the worm?"

"Yes," the kids said.

"Very good, Lucy. Isn't it very good?"

"Yes!"

Lucy smiled and Mrs. Boyden smiled and Miss Jude licked a gold star and put it on the painting in the upper corner. "A gold star for Lucy."

David Bumgartner had painted the next one.

"Hmmm," Miss Jude said, studying it. "It looks like a fish to me."

"A whale," said David, who suddenly covered his mouth because he'd not been called on.

Mrs. Boyden smiled, for the Bumgartner boy was learning.

"Oh, I see the whale now," said Miss Jude. "Oh yes indeed. And is that the whale spout?"

"Yes, ma'am."

"Class, do you see the water spurting up?"

"Yes, Miss Jude."

"Whales have spouts which spurt water. Not only is your painting recognizable, but it's taken from real life. Very, very good."

Tim Myerly, the new boy, started to clap, which caught on. All of the kids except Scotty and Carole clapped. Carole didn't because she was next up and all she could think about was what Miss Jude would say. Scotty refused to clap. He didn't think much of the whale. He would later tell Claire, "A dumb whale."

Carole Staley had covered her paper—a sun that blazed,

her ocean blue and bright. She had painted the boldest mountains, violet and indigo with streaks of dark purple. And while
she'd never seen a mountain, she'd seen *National Geographic*
magazines and specials on public television, and, finally, she was
Carole who could imagine anything.

Miss Jude looked at the painting. She turned to the class
and said with a smile, "Who painted this one?"

Carole raised her hand. The class turned to look at her.
Scotty looked down at his hands. He noticed traces of paint on
his fingers, under his nails. He thought of how he had scrubbed
and scrubbed that afternoon. Paint doesn't come off me, he
thought. It just doesn't come off.

When Miss Jude turned back to the painting, the class followed. Carole looked at Scotty, who smiled his congratulations.

Miss Jude said, "Carole, mountains aren't this color."

The room became still.

"They're never purple. Isn't that right, class?"

"Yes, Miss Jude."

"But should we give Carole a gold star anyway?" And
before the class could answer, Miss Jude said, "I think we
should." Then she licked the star.

Scotty looked to his painting partner. He noticed rapid
movement in her stomach muscles; her face turned a bright,
flush red. The tears didn't roll out or drip down—they shot
out like bullets, splattering the table. When Carole Staley folded
her arms and put her head down on the desk, a sound broke
out of her, a scream.

Scotty couldn't help but wish he was sitting elsewhere.

Miss Jude stopped. She looked at Mrs. Boyden, who waited
patiently for a time, then spoke: "Part of being an artist is
learning to accept constructive criticism. That's part of making

art." Mrs. Boyden meant those words to be helpful but they only caused Carole to sob louder.

Scotty's stomach began to hurt.

As she led Carole from the classroom, Mrs. Boyden signaled Miss Jude to continue.

She critiqued with great care now—gentle, always encouraging. (One student in tears and it could be explained as an overly sensitive child; two or more devastated students and she'd be held accountable.)

So Miss Jude praised Bobette Daley's barn with barnyard animals. The proportions were all wrong, the animals were all pink, but Miss Jude praised her all the same and gave the gold star.

"No cows are pink," Scotty wanted to say.

Patrick O'Meara's painting of a fireman was next. Miss Jude heaped praise on Patrick even though he painted the fireman with a blue face.

"No firemen got blue faces," Scotty wanted to say.

Ruth Rethman's green pizza got a gold star because, "I look at this and I know exactly what it is and that's good."

Gold stars for everyone.

When Miss Jude got to Scotty's black-and-white painting, she looked at it long. And Scotty had this thought: If she liked those other paintings, then she surely has to love me.

Miss Jude looked at his painting for what felt like hours. He knew he'd impressed her for she had no words. As Miss Jude moved closer to his painting, Scotty prepared for praise.

Miss Jude thought about abstract art and how she hated it. Suddenly worried about the length of her silence and knowing she had to say something, Miss Jude turned around and asked, "Who painted this one?"

"Scotty Ocean painted it," Mrs. Boyden said as she returned to the classroom.

"Isn't your mother a painter?"

Scotty nodded proudly.

Miss Jude looked back at the painting, and not knowing what to say, blurted out, "What is it?"

Scotty smiled but didn't answer. He remembered his mother had told him that paintings have many meanings, that it was up to each individual to interpret.

"Scotty," Mrs. Boyden said, "Miss Jude asked you a question."

"I know."

"What is it?"

"It's a real thing."

Miss Jude began to make out the shape of a face. "Is it a painting of you?"

"Yes."

Miss Jude looked back at the painting; she looked at Scotty. "Well, then what is that part right there?"

Scotty stood and pointed below his belt.

The painting suddenly came into focus for Miss Jude. At the top of the paper, painted in a squiggly fashion, was a face. Below the face, a boy's chest with circles for nipples. And below that . . .

The children had begun to move about, whisper, and squirm, after Scotty pointed to his penis. Before chaos could break out, Mrs. Boyden said, "Okay, class, let's thank Miss Jude for her kind gift of time and talent."

The kids applauded meekly. It was time for recess. They knew it. Mrs. Boyden excused them and they giggled and tittered about Scotty's nude portrait as they gathered up their coats and mittens and ran outside. Scotty waited until the others had left. While Miss Jude spoke in a whisper to Mrs. Boyden, Scotty walked slowly down the aisle, his hands lightly touching the tops of the other desks. I've dazzled her, he thought. She can hardly look me in the eye. Before he left the classroom, Miss Jude stopped him.

"Scotty, may I keep this for a while?"

He hesitated.

"May I? It's a most . . . uhm . . . interesting piece of work. May I . . . uhm . . . borrow it?"

"You can *borrow* it."

"Thank you."

"I get it back, right?"

"Of course."

"And I get the gold star, right?"

Scotty described the painting as he helped Claire set the table for Thanksgiving dinner. It had been two days since he'd painted it, and he knew, deep down, it was his best painting.

"It sounds like a masterpiece," she said as she folded napkins.

"Oh yes."

"Maybe it could be framed."

"Oh, yes."

Scotty decided he would send it to his mother.

When Carole Staley returned to class the Monday after Thanksgiving, she ate her usual peanut butter and jelly sandwich out of her Barbie lunch pail, and she seemed to have recovered nicely from the art class the week before.

Scotty, too, resumed his old patterns, pulling her pigtails

and avoiding her kisses. All seemed fine; all had been forgotten.

But at the end of the day, Scotty approached Mrs. Boyden
and said, "Did Miss Jude bring back my picture?"

Mrs. Boyden smiled and said, "Not yet."

The boy will forget eventually, she thought, in that beautiful way all children forget.

For days, though, Scotty persisted, always asking politely,
and always accepting the news of "Not yet" with a hopeful
grin.

At night when the phone rang, he wanted it to be Miss
Jude calling. "Scotty is the best artist ever," he imagined she
would say.

But she never called.

Days passed; soon it was December, and Scotty began to wonder if he'd ever see his painting again. He asked at the end of
each day and Mrs. Boyden kept repeating "Any day now."
Once, during Art time, he tried to re-create the painting, but
as hard as he tried, it was not to be recaptured.

On the last day before Christmas break, Scotty stood in front
of Mrs. Boyden.

"Have a nice Christmas, Scotty," Mrs. Boyden said. She
looked down and when she looked back up, Scotty was still
standing there. "How can I help you?"

"My painting."

"Miss Jude really must have liked it. Everybody got the
gold star. But yours is the only one she kept."

"But . . ."

"Next year, Scotty."

"But . . ."

"Next year." Then she smiled. "I hope you and your family have a wonderful holiday."

(17)

On the way home, Scotty came upon Tom Conway, who was waiting for him at the top of Woodland Avenue.

Earlier that day, at lunch, when everyone showed everyone else what they were eating, Tom Conway refused to open his *Rat Patrol* lunch pail. Throughout the day he carried it with him, even into the bathroom, which made Scotty curious.

But now Tom Conway was gesturing for Scotty to approach, which he did. Tom unlatched the lunch box and showed Scotty the contents: a Baggie full of crushed Oreo cookies, three butterscotch candies, and a hand grenade.

Seeing the grenade, Scotty took off running. He heard the high-pitched sound of the grenade in the air; he felt it coming close. Diving like a soldier in the movies, he covered his imaginary helmet with his hands, shut his eyes, held his breath, prayed.

Then he heard laughing.

Tom Conway stepped on Scotty's rear end as he walked over him, his lunch pail swinging, the sound of the grenade rolling around inside.

"Ho, ho, ho," Tom said, as if Santa Claus.

.   .   .

That night at dinner the Judge told his children that he had good news. "I spoke to your mother." The Judge paused. He wiped his mouth with his napkin. "She called me at the courthouse. I have some news you might be interested in."

All eyes were on him.

"She'll be home for Christmas."

It took a moment to sink in. Maggie smiled, Claire had questions, and Scotty slid off his chair, crawled to the center of the kitchen where he proceeded to jump up and down. Then he launched into a variation of his seven dance. And as he danced, he thought, See what happens when you're good.

CHRISTMAS

(1)

The Ocean house had never been so clean: carpets vacuumed, toilets scrubbed, the kitchen floor mopped, the refrigerator defrosted; new outfits for the children, showers for all; a six-foot-tall Christmas tree decorated with blinking lights, stockings hung from oldest to youngest—everything was ready, and they were hours ahead of schedule. The Oceans sat around waiting. Scotty was especially careful not to make a mess.

(2)

Sent in to get the Christmas cookies, Scotty found the platter covered in cellophane on the kitchen counter. The cookies were cut in various shapes: a Christmas wreath, a Christmas tree, a candy cane. Some of the cookies had been colored a seasonal green, some Santa Claus red—the remaining majority were a tannish white, browned at the edges. Claire had baked the day before while Maggie and Scotty decorated. The wreath cookies had green frosting and were peppered with little red-hot candies, the Christmas tree cookies had colored sprinkles, and the candy canes had been given uneven frosting stripes by Maggie, who hadn't yet mastered the frosting gun.

As Scotty was about to lift the cookie tray, the doorbell rang. He stood frozen. He held his breath as the front door was opened. He heard the muffle of greetings, the happy voices. He checked his clothes. He wore his first suit—blue, like his father's—a light blue dress shirt, Buster Brown shoes, black socks, and a red clip-on tie, a first, too. His father wore a red tie and Scotty wished they had on different colors.

"Wear a different one, Dad," he'd whispered earlier that evening.

"No, Scotty. This way we're the same."

Scotty had pulled at his out of frustration. Then he ran to the bathroom, climbed on the toilet seat, and checked to see if the tie had remained straight.

Now, he checked the tie again. "It'll do," he said. Then he lifted the cookie tray as high as he could. (He was determined not to drop it.) He made his way into the living room where his father, his sisters, his maternal grandparents, and most important, Joan Ocean, who stood in the doorway with sacks of presents at her side, all looked his way.

There was plenty of smiling and Scotty could feel all eyes were on him. He lowered the tray to the coffee table. He made a big sigh like "Whew."

"Don't you look nice," Joan said.

Scotty walked toward her and extended his hand, which Joan shook.

"You look like a little man."

What Scotty saw before him, he decided, was definitely new and improved—Joan wore a black dress, tight fitting, and bright red lipstick; her cheeks were colored and her hair pulled back simply, revealing ruby drop earrings, which dangled.

Scotty wanted to sit next to his mother. But Maggie had taken the spot, so he waited near the Christmas tree. Surely she'll look over at the tree, he thought.

Scotty's clothes itched. Normally he'd make a scene. Wearing clothes such as these, he'd moan and fidget—but not on Christmas Eve 1969. She was in her living room tonight and Scotty would behave his very best, give her no reason to flee again.

His grandfather and the Judge brought in the sacks of gifts. This year Scotty didn't run to stack his up to see how high they would stand. He gave no indication of caring. He sat, a cookie held daintily in his hand, waiting his turn to speak. Only one part of his hair stuck up.

When Maggie went to the bathroom, Scotty took her place. He leaned toward Joan's ear, cupped his hand so only she could hear. Her hair smelled of shampoo and cigarettes.

"You back for good?" Scotty asked his mother, in a whisper.

Joan smiled, but didn't say anything. She squeezed his knee with her available hand.

Before going to midnight Mass, everyone opened one present. Scotty went first but only because he was youngest. Joan suggested he open the gift from her parents. So he did. It came in two boxes. In the first, there was an assortment of various wood shapes. In the second, various tools, boy-size.

"To build things," Scotty said. He hugged his mother.

"They're from Grandma Dottie and Grandpa Jim."

He crossed the room to his grandparents. He shook his grandfather's hand and kissed near his grandmother's ear. The grandmother leaned forward to kiss him, her lips bright red with Christmas lipstick, and Scotty turned his head at the last minute. She planted a big smooch on his cheek and his face contracted more the harder she pressed. He saw his father sitting in the corner, watching the festivities with a quiet joy. Their eyes made contact, the men, and they both knew.

She's back was what they knew.

She's back.

When Scotty got released from his grandmother's clutches, Maggie laughed then quickly covered her mouth, remembering it was Christmas and you don't laugh at someone on Christmas.

"You have lips on your face," Claire said.

Joan had a handkerchief. She wiped Scotty's cheek.

"I used to leave my lips all over your grandfather's face. There was a time when all we did was kiss," the grandmother said. She smiled. The grandfather smiled but wondered if this was something Scotty needed to know. Then he leaned forward and explained the use of certain tools.

"You know the hammer."

"Yeah."

"You know the screwdriver. Now this here is a leveler."

Scotty held it. Part metal, part wood, the leveler had a thin tube filled with green-yellow liquid. In the tube an air bubble moved from side to side as Scotty tilted it every which way.

"You want the bubble to be in the middle. That way you got everything balanced, everything equal."

Scotty nodded as if he understood. As Maggie tore off the

wrapping of her present, Scotty looked to his mother. Joan smiled as Maggie squealed. She had given Maggie the game Mystery Date. You're back, Scotty thought.

She's back, Joan Ocean is back.

As they put on their winter coats to go to church, Joan announced suddenly, "I want Scotty to open one more gift."

She extended a small package.

Scotty carefully tore away the paper. He opened the plastic case. Inside was a boy's wristwatch with luminous hands.

"Oh boy," Scotty said.

"So you can see it in the dark," Joan said as she helped him put it on his wrist.

"I can tell time," Scotty said.

"Of course you can."

Outside, a thin layer of snow covered the driveway and the stoop. As the family headed to the cars for the ride to church, Scotty could make out the silhouette of the mailbox. He reminded himself, *Be sure not to lick it*. Not going through that again, he whispered to himself. Lesson learned.

In the car, Scotty rode in front between the Judge and Joan, but closer to Joan. He pushed in the cigarette lighter. When it clicked, he looked to her and she nodded and he pulled it out and held it up. She leaned forward, her cigarette between her lips, and Scotty heard it begin to sizzle. His mother inhaled and he slid the lighter back into place.

At the church, luminarias lined the sidewalks and the walkways leading to the church.

"Who would think that a grocery sack, a handful of sand, and a cheap candle could make such a light?" the Judge wondered aloud. "Who would think?"

Those attending the service saw Joan enter with the Oceans, and all agreed that she'd never looked better.

Scotty stood next to his mother. He wanted to hold her hand. He forgot about his painting and how she would love it. For the first time in weeks his memory became like an Etch-A-Sketch freshly shaken—he was wiped clean.

During the service, all eyes were on the Ocean family. The Judge wore his best blue suit. Scotty's sisters each wore a dress made by their other grandmother, a widow, living in Florida. Dresses that neither of the girls would ever wear again. But the picture would be taken and sent south after the New Year. In previous years, when the girls were younger, the dresses were often identical. This year, in honor of the individual, and due to the definite chasm that had grown between the sisters physically, each dress had its own style. The fabrics went well together and while the girls weren't happy, for a night they would suffer. For a night, for this night even Scotty would not complain. He didn't fidget. He had no trouble staying awake.

That night Scotty lay in his bed, his eyes open. He knew he'd slept some of the time, he didn't know how long, what with the outside still dark. A whistly wind blew against the storm windows of his bedroom. Scotty held back the curtain with his hand. He saw winter outside. He saw the frozen glass, the glaze of ice on trees, branches standing brittle, waiting for warmer days. Poor trees, Scotty thought. Wish it could be warm out there like it is in here.

Too excited to sleep, Scotty dropped feet first to the floor. He put on socks that he found in the top drawer of his dresser. "Hope they match," he said to himself as he opened the door and crept down the hall. He pushed open his parents' door. The only light came from the glow of the Judge's alarm clock. Scotty practically leapt over the lump under the sheets that was his father. He came down on the other side; he came between his parents and he landed as inconspicuously as any seven-year-old boy could. He waited for the mattress to go still from the aftershocks. He rolled away from his father toward his mother when he found that side of the bed to be empty, the pillow fresh. He felt for her; he peered over the side to see if she'd rolled onto the floor. He checked under the bed. He slid open the closet door.

"Dad," he finally said, poking the Judge gently in the back. "Dad."

"Hmmmm," said the Judge, more asleep than not.

"Where's Mom?" Scotty whispered.

In a voice too loud, the Judge replied, "She doesn't want to live here anymore."

Scotty did not breathe. He felt no noticeable pain. He rolled off the bed and walked quietly back to his room. He climbed in his bed, determined to not seem surprised.

He didn't move for a long time.

As he lay there, it was as if a vacuum hose had been inserted down his throat, for he could not speak, and everything vital, everything pure, got sucked out, everything sucked out until finally only his heart remained; its veins and ventricles and arteries clung to his ribs. He imagined the high-pitched sound a vacuum makes when a piece of plastic or a baby sock clogs the passageway. Then something shifted, the whine of the vacuum kicked to a higher pitch, the heart began to stretch, to be pulled, and finally it was ripped out and went screaming down the tube, gone.

(3)

In the morning, after a breakfast of coffee cake, the Judge and his children opened their remaining presents. Maggie was the last to notice Scotty's lack of enthusiasm, the way he slowly opened gifts. "You've lost the Christmas spirit," she said, as she emptied her Christmas stocking on the living room carpet. Inside she found Barbie's Accessory Pak and the Barbie Hair Fair, which included one Barbie head with short hair, a wiglet, ringlets, ponytail, and extra wig.

She sighed and said, "No more Barbie! Please!"

Then Claire carefully removed the wrapping off a book. It was a biography on Thomas Jefferson, whom both the Judge and Claire admired. By coincidence, Jefferson's daughter had taken over the running of Jefferson's house after his wife had died. The Judge apologized for the inference. But Claire said, "There are many differences between Patsy Jefferson and me. The most obvious is that they had slaves."

Over the coming weeks, and always after Claire had ordered Maggie and Scotty to shovel the driveway or take out the trash, Maggie would say, "Yes, master."

Claire got upset at the insinuation. She was no slave driver: She was doing the best she could.

The Judge insisted Maggie stop it. So Maggie substituted Mother for master, which Scotty began to imitate. "Yes, Mother. Okay, Mother." Occasionally this would make Claire cry, but mainly she ignored them, clearing her throat in an intentional manner, and assigned them more chores.

As the Judge prepared to open his gift, Claire said, "Explain it, Scotty."

Scotty said nothing.

"It was your idea," Claire reminded him.

The commercial had been Scotty's favorite during the holiday season. Santa Claus riding the Norelco Tripleheader shaver as if it were a sled down a snowy mountain. Santa delivering toys to all the good boys and girls on a razor. Every time the commercial played, Scotty lunged toward the TV and followed the razor with his finger as Santa rode it through the snow.

When he and his sisters had been dropped at Kmart to do their shopping, Scotty announced his idea. Anything to soften the Judge's face had been Scotty's thinking. A simple hug felt like a bed of nails being pressed to his face. It seemed like the perfect gift.

"It's rechargeable, Daddy," Maggie said.

The Judge seemed pleased.

Scotty started to open his gift after his sisters insisted.

"It's what you asked for," the Judge said.

Scotty couldn't remember having asked for anything. He was in a fog. Everything felt as if it were covered in maple syrup. Was he the only one upset?

"Did you hear Dad, Scotty?" Claire asked. "He said it's what you asked for."

That meant Scotty better like it.

"Hurry up."

Scotty finished tearing off the wrapping paper. The gift was an official NFL boy's Minnesota Vikings uniform. In a few weeks the Vikings and the Kansas City Chiefs would play in Super Bowl IV.

Inside the box were a helmet, shoulder pads, padded pants, and a purple and white jersey. Included were two sets of iron-on numbers.

"Gee, I wonder what number Scotty will want," Maggie said.

Not only had his predictability become a source of comfort to his family; it was becoming a source of ridicule. They knew what he'd eat; they knew his favorite colors, his favorite TV shows, the commercials he perked up for, his routine. He could be anticipated, countered. He didn't understand that he was being taken for granted, but he sensed that something must change.

"Say thank you," Claire urged, but the Judge gestured for her to be silent.

"I saw that," Scotty wanted to say. "I see everything." He lifted the helmet and unwrapped the plastic that surrounded it. His fingers traced the white horns. The brightness of the Minnesota Vikings purple was as brilliant as a grape gum ball—he pulled the helmet over his head. The gray plastic face guard had two bars, like a quarterback's helmet. Protection and visibility were both important. Two plastic holes muffled the sound.

"Can you hear us?" Claire asked.

Yes, I can hear you, Scotty thought. But he said nothing.

"I think he likes it, Dad," Maggie said.

The Judge smiled and said, "Well, it's what he wanted."

Tom Conway knocked on the door around ten that morning, out of breath with the news that they'd been given a collie puppy.

Before Scotty showed Tom what he got, he put on the helmet. Only then did Scotty begin to show his other toys. "This is Fort Cheyenne. Indians and Cowboys fight their fights. The river divides them." They assembled his new Hot Wheels track. Long orange plastic strips held together by purple connectors. Scotty had two loop-the-loops and he and Tom stretched track all over the living room, and played until Tom got bored.

After Tom Conway left, Scotty continued to wear the helmet. He even ate with it on. Maggie complained that the Christmas meal should be eaten in the best conditions. "Scotty's helmet makes it impossible for me to take this meal seriously."

Claire spoke gently. "You're getting gravy on the face mask part."

Scotty did not care. He wanted to wear it.

The Judge, hating the bickering, said in a resolute voice, the same voice he used when sentencing a criminal, "It's a great day to wear a helmet."

Victory. The helmet remained on and Scotty continued eating, occasionally leaving traces of food on the face guard. The chin strap made chewing difficult. He unsnapped it but the helmet began slipping all about so he snapped it back on. It made a loud *click* sound when he fastened it. No one looked at him, though. No one watched how he struggled: his bottom jaw unable to move, the top jaw and the head above it rising up and down. But it was good. Scotty was safe, the Minnesota Vikings helmet on his head, shoulder pads tied tightly, prepared in case. In case the roof caved in. In case a scout drove by and the team needed another player. In case a bullet from Vietnam came shooting through the back door. Scotty was prepared.

And so he waited.

It would be a week before school resumed.

By the third day after Christmas, all interest in the new toys had been exhausted. Television took up most of Scotty's time. He watched his favorite shows—*Bonanza, My Three Sons, Family Affair. The Courtship of Eddie's Father.*

New and Improved Tide laundry detergent was being advertised. New and Improved toilet paper. New and Improved soap.

Scotty stared blankly at the TV. He never told his dad or his sisters or even Tom Conway the whereabouts of his heart. He knew it was gone.

But he had his brain and that was what really mattered. With his brain he would outsmart his heart.

OTHER MOTHERS

(1)

Bev Fowler held her new Betsy Wetsy in one hand and the Betsy Wetsy tote bag in the other. Pushing up her black horn-rimmed glasses, Bev said, "I like that she drinks, cries real tears, and wets her diaper." She lifted up Betsy Wetsy for everyone to see.

"Make her cry," Scotty called out.

Bev inserted a pink baby bottle filled with water into the doll's rubber mouth.

"Thank you, Bev," Mrs. Boyden said.

"Make her cry!"

"That's enough, Scotty." Then turning to Bev, Mrs. Boyden said, "Only a good girl would get such a nice gift. Have a seat."

"But in a minute she'll wet her pants. . . ."

"Very good, Bev. You'll make a wonderful mother one day. Next."

Bev reluctantly moved to her desk, where later, unnoticed, she would change Betsy's diaper.

"Who wants to go next?"

Hands shot above heads—fingers stretching—class members eager to show and tell. Scotty waited quietly with his arms folded. He wanted to go last.

Other boys couldn't wait. Richard Hibbs showed his new underwater G.I. Joe; Dan Burkhett the G.I. Joe motorcycle with sidecar, and Chip Fisher the G.I. Joe jeep and trailer with lighted searchlight.

"Good boys, all of you," Mrs. Boyden said. "And once again G.I. Joe seems to be very popular."

Shari Tussey showed a blue saucer sled with yellow plastic handgrips. Ruth Rethman got a Kenner Easy Bake oven, which was too big for show-and-tell, so she held the torn page from the Sears catalog. She told how she'd already made brownies and devil's food cake. Jimmy Lamson got Feeley-Meeley and the Game of Life; he couldn't decide which to show, so he brought both.

"I'm lucky to have so many good students. Yes, I'm lucky."

Throughout the classroom, those who hadn't been called on switched arms, and continued to wave and stretch, eager for their turn.

Brian and Harry Hammer, the twins, went next. They each held a walkie-talkie. They pulled out the antennas, which extended almost two feet. "These are deluxe ones," Brian said.

For their demonstration, Brian remained standing in front of the class while Harry went out into the hall.

"Can you read me?" Brian said. "Over."

Harry's voice came back with static. "I can read you. Over."

"Where are you? Over."

"I'm in the hallway. Over."

"Uhm. Can you still read me? Over."

"I can still read you. Over."

Mrs. Boyden told Brian to call Harry back.

"Mrs. Boyden said for you to come back."

Harry returned and some of the kids clapped.

"You must have been *very* good," Mrs. Boyden said. And the Hammer twins smiled and took their seats.

Then Mrs. Boyden called on Scotty.

"I'm not ready," he said.

"Well, it's your turn."

"No."

"I hope we don't run out of time."

Time.

Scotty glanced at the clock on the wall, the red arm circling the clock face. He looked at his watch with the glow-in-the-dark hands. His classmates were waiting, and Scotty worried as he watched the second hand tick. If he didn't show his favorite gift now, he might not get to show at all. So he grabbed the grocery sack at his feet and sped down the aisle. In front of the class he lifted the Minnesota Vikings helmet out of the grocery sack. He put it on his head and snapped the chin strap. He pointed to the helmet. He smacked at it with an open hand. Carole Staley giggled. Her father had been a football player in college, and she liked football. Then Scotty held the jersey over his head. He lifted up the plastic shoulder pads and the football pants with padding sewn into the knees.

"You must've been good, too," Mrs. Boyden said.

Scotty leaned over the nearest desk, as if inviting Craig Hunt to pound the helmet. Craig took a whap and Mrs. Boyden said, "Now boys."

Scotty turned and ran, his head down, and thumped into the concrete brick wall. He looked up, dazed slightly from the collision, and did a dramatic drop to the floor where he lay motionless. He squeezed his eyes shut and strained to listen for any reaction he was getting. But the helmet's small ear holes made it difficult to hear. So Scotty stood, only to discover the class had gone on. Christine Bettis was standing in front of the class demonstrating her *Chitty Chitty Bang Bang* car. With the touch of the brake lever, the colorful red and yellow wings flicked out. Some kids went "Oooo."

Scotty made it back to his seat where he continued to wear his helmet in protest.

The rest of the children showed their favorite toys. Leann Callahan held up her Peggy Fleming ice skates. Tom Conway told about the collie puppy their father got them. The Conways named their puppy Lassie. "Because she looks just like Lassie," Tom said. Craig Hunt, who went with his family to California for the holidays, told about his trip to Disneyland. He passed around pictures of the Disney castle and of Craig standing with Mickey Mouse in front of the Matterhorn.

As Craig was finishing, a knock came on the classroom door. Mrs. Boyden opened the door and said to the unseen person, "We've been waiting for you." Tim Myerly's mother, dressed in a pink parka, entered the room holding up a cage wrapped with an insulated blanket.

Tim Myerly stood and moved to the front of the class. His mother leaned over and whispered in his ear. Tim told the class to close their eyes. Scotty pretended to but squinted. He saw Tim's mother unwrap the blanket.

"Okay, open."

When the others opened their eyes, they saw what Scotty

had already seen—in the cage sat a green and yellow bird with a black beak the size of a grown man's thumb.

"Does it talk?" was the first question.

"No—but it sings."

"And it likes TV," the mother added.

While the other kids looked at the bird, Scotty studied the mother. She wore a pink ribbon in her hair and her lips were made up to match. She was short, with black hair, wavy like cake frosting, ivory skin, and large, brown, Bambi-like eyes. She was the prettiest mother he had ever seen.

Scotty blurted out the first question that came to him. "Does the bird get lonely?"

Mrs. Boyden glared at Scotty. Not only did he not raise his hand, but he was still wearing his helmet.

Tim and his mother looked around for the person who had spoken.

Scotty said it again: "Does the bird get lonely?"

Tim Myerly stood motionless. He was stumped by Scotty's question. He knew his bird's age, its natural habitat, and favorite foods. He knew every fact imaginable, for his father had drilled him on the facts. But he knew nothing of feelings. Feelings were never considered, and the longer Tim stood unable to speak, the more Scotty wanted to look at Tim's mother. Tim turned to her. She turned to Scotty and, without acknowledging the helmet, said something.

The helmet muffled her voice. Scotty stopped breathing in an attempt to hear better, but he didn't catch a word.

"We try to give Tim's bird the best home imaginable" was what she said.

Scotty nodded. Whatever she said must be right.

Then Mrs. Boyden allowed the students in small groups to

approach the cage and get a closer look. Scotty stayed seated. Mrs. Myerly sweetly answered the students' questions. He studied how her mouth moved, and when it was his turn, he felt too shy to move toward her.

At noon Leann Callahan's new lunch pail provided the boys with conversation material. Dome shaped, the pail was painted to look like a loaf of bread. The thermos was a replica of a Campbell's tomato soup can. No one had ever seen a lunch pail quite like it before.

"Stupid," Dan Burkhett said. "A loaf of bread. What a stupid thing."

While the other boys laughed, Scotty (with his helmet still strapped to his head) sat across from Tim Myerly. In the weeks since Tim had moved to Iowa, the two of them had never really talked. And now Scotty didn't know how to start. He looked to see what was packed in Tim's Snoopy lunch pail: Snack Pack pudding, a bag of Fritos, a banana with the blue and white Chiquita sticker still on, a bologna sandwich, and a Twinkie. Tim's thermos was filled with chicken noodle soup. He also had a milk card, which got him a small square carton each lunch. That day Tim had chosen chocolate milk, which he sipped through a white plastic straw.

Scotty broke off bite-size portions of his peanut butter and jelly sandwich and fed himself through his face mask. He had his usual bare-bones lunch. The daily peanut butter and jelly sandwich on Wonder bread, a Baggie full of Highland potato chips, a small, bruised apple, and a handful of butterscotch candies.

Not knowing what to say exactly, Scotty proposed a trade.

"My butterscotch candies for your Twinkie."

"No," Tim Myerly said.

"Okay," Scotty said. "My potato chips for your pudding."

"No way," Tim Myerly said.

"Your sticker for my candy?" Scotty asked.

But Tim took the Chiquita sticker, peeled it off his banana, and stuck it smack in the middle of his forehead.

It became clear—Tim Myerly didn't want to trade.

Later, while holding up flash cards and reviewing subtraction, Mrs. Boyden asked Scotty for a third time to remove his helmet. When he didn't, Mrs. Boyden moved quickly to the back where Scotty was sitting. Scotty watched as she headed toward him, but since he hadn't heard her, he wasn't prepared. She grabbed at his helmet, pulled it off with such force that it hurt his ears. "See me after class," she snapped. She took the helmet to the front of the room, placed it under her desk, and continued with her lesson plan.

"Why is subtraction important, boys and girls?" Mrs. Boyden's flash of anger had left her students stunned. "Subtraction evens things out."

At the end of the day, Scotty waited at Mrs. Boyden's desk. He held out his hands. "Helmet," he seemed to be saying.

"Of course."

She reached under her desk and lifted it up.

He quickly pulled it over his head, snapped the chin strap, and said, "You can't keep taking things from me." He turned and marched out of the room.

.   .   .

Mrs. Boyden knew that he was referring to his self-portrait. And she didn't tell him what she had learned. On New Year's Day, she bumped into Miss Clarissa Jude at the home of a mutual friend. She told Miss Jude that her students still talk about the wonderful day she came to visit. Miss Jude said that periodic visits to young artists in schools was part of her "giving back." Mrs. Boyden mentioned Scotty Ocean's naked self-portrait. Miss Jude paused and said with a smile, "I really had no choice. I tore the painting into little pieces and put it in the trash."

"Oh," Mrs. Boyden said.

"I thought, Someone has to take a stand. So, that was that." Then Miss Jude said she'd be happy to come back anytime.

Mrs. Boyden said nothing to Miss Jude, but she had thoughts on the subject: I might not know anything about art, but never again will you teach my class.

Scotty continued to wear his football helmet to school. And because she felt badly about the painting, Mrs. Boyden permitted it. But when, on the third day, Chip Fisher showed up with his Kansas City Chiefs helmet and Tom Conway wore his father's military helmet, Mrs. Boyden knew she had to take action. She asked the three boys to stay for a moment after the others went to lunch. "It appears Scotty has started a trend."

Yes, I have, he thought.

"Soon every boy will be wearing a helmet. And we can't have that, can we?"

"Yes, we can," Scotty said.

Mrs. Boyden smiled. "No, Scotty, I'm afraid we can't. In the future you boys need to leave your helmets at home."

(2)

"Make the bad good," the Judge would say. *"Make the bad good!"* For he believed there were positive aspects to any unpleasant situation. Claire had her doubts. She read the paper. She watched the TV news. There was real evidence of evil. There was Vietnam and pollution. Scotty knew enough to know that Claire was usually right.

But the Judge knew that with Joan gone, for instance, his children would get to know him better. He was right. They saw a new side to him immediately—his playful use of language. If he promised to do something, he would say, "You can COD." It meant: count on Dad. He had other odd terms for things. Even the toilet had a special name. As he headed for the bathroom, he loved to call out, "I'm going to go sit on the throne."

"Like he's some kind of king," Maggie would complain.

"You're just upset about your new name," Claire said.

The Judge had given them all nicknames and Maggie was not pleased. Claire became Clarinet, Maggie was called Magpie, and Scotty—Scotch Tape.

"It's a phase," Claire argued.

"But *Magpie*? I hate Magpie."

"He's upset about Mom. Let him have some fun."

"But why these stupid names?"

Claire explained. "Clarinet because I'm music to his ears. . . ."

"And why Magpie?"

"Well, Magpie because . . ."

"See, you don't know."

"Magpie is an incessantly talkative bird."

"So? I don't talk a lot," Maggie whined. "Not that much at all. Okay, maybe I do. But that's because nobody is saying things, you know, things that need to be said. *I'm* the one who says things. Scotty doesn't say anything. . . ."

It was true. Scotty had been mostly quiet since Christmas. He didn't have much to say. He stared at his family during mealtimes and his teachers during class time with a blank expression, as if the rest of the world were speaking another language.

TV brought a particular comfort.

He began most mornings with *Captain Kangaroo*. He waited for Mr. Moose to say the secret word. When the word was spoken, hundreds of Ping-Pong balls rained down from above.

He liked the animated tapping foot at the start of *My Three Sons,* the lighting of the fuse on *Mission: Impossible,* and always (he never missed, in fact) the opening credits of *Hawaii Five-O,* where he moved to the percussive and brass-filled theme song until the giant wave filled the screen, and then he pretended as if he were being washed away.

His new favorite commercial was for Purina Puppy Chow. As a miniature chuck wagon with its red-and-white-checkered tarp sped across a clean kitchen floor, a shaggy white sheepdog chased after in determined pursuit. Then, suddenly, and to the confusion of the dog, the wagon disappeared into the floorboard of the kitchen cabinetry.

Wouldn't it be great to disappear like that?

His mother had.

If there had been any residual hope of her return, it was erased with the news that Joan had moved to Iowa City, ninety miles due east of Des Moines, taken a tiny studio apartment, and enrolled in a broad variety of college courses at the university.

On her way out of town, she had stopped by the house. She stayed in the car as her three children, one at a time, got in to say good-bye. Scotty went last.

In her talk with Claire, Joan revealed the most: She was going to Iowa City to get a master's degree in something wonderful, anything but art. Her paintings had been put in storage. She hoped never to look at them again. Then she told Claire, "You're the smartest girl ever."

She told Maggie she was the prettiest girl ever. "So please," Joan warned, "be careful with boys."

She told Scotty she would miss him most, that he was her favorite man.

She asked each of them to kiss her, and they did, except for Scotty, who didn't feel like kissing.

While all this happened, the Judge busied himself making a dinner. He had become obsessed with the idea of the family meal. His knowledge of the grocery stores in the area had increased. He knew where to get the best buy. He cut coupons from the newspaper. And on Saturday afternoons, he loaded up the Dodge with Scotty and his sisters and they spent long hours driving to Hy-Vee, then to Safeway, to Hinky Dinky, to Dahl's. One store had a better price on milk, another had the freshest bread, another the cheapest meat.

Everyone had their particular tasks during dinner preparations. Claire mixed the Jiffy corn muffins or the blueberry muffins. She supervised the baking of Tater Tots and wrapped potatoes in aluminum foil. She opened the canned fruits and vegetables. She learned the proper mix of ingredients for the fruit salad dressing.

Maggie's job, the hardest, was to wait at the Judge's side to assist him on any need that might arise. "Salt," he might say, in a sudden panic, "I need salt!"

Scotty poured the drinks and was responsible for keeping the Judge's water bottle filled. "Always refill it after using it; that way I'll always have water."

Because the Judge wanted everything to go right, inevitably something always went wrong. Scotty spilled a glass of milk, Maggie burned the bread, or the oven wasn't turned on at the right time. The Judge would rage.

Scotty learned to stand in the corner of the kitchen near the phone during these times. He learned that if he didn't move, there was a good chance the Judge wouldn't yell at him, a good chance the Judge would forget he was even there.

Monday night meals were baked or barbecued chicken. Tuesday night—spaghetti.

Wednesday nights the Judge attended Kiwanis, a men's fellowship group that met at Baker's Cafeteria. On those nights individual Stouffer's pot pies—chicken, turkey, or beef—sat thawing. Claire heated the oven, Maggie set the table, and when the pot pies were served, Scotty ate only the crust.

On Thursday nights, after a meal of pork chops or a pork roast, and after all homework was completed, they would clean the house in preparation for the hired cleaning lady who would come each Friday. They never saw her—she was always finished before they returned home from school—but they loved swinging open the door and finding everything in place, everything vacuumed. Friday night meals would be hamburgers usually or steak if the week had gone well.

Saturdays usually consisted of leftovers.

Sunday night they would go out to eat, McDonald's usually, sometimes King's Food Host or the A & W.

For the Judge, dinner was the most important time of the day. He believed, and said it often, "it's important that we do things as a family."

(3)

Since the New Year, Judge Ocean, his two girls, and Scotty had been regularly attending St. Stephen's Episcopal Church. Each week they took their place in the second pew, where they had a fine view of the altar and the forty-foot steel-beamed cross that hung from nearly invisible wires. The Oceans always arrived early and kneeled together in prayer, with the Judge remaining on his knees until the first notes of the processional hymn blared on the church's organ.

That first week Scotty squirmed about in his polyester Sunday best, looking around and such, but, halfway through the service, he looked back and saw something. Immediately he began to behave.

Claire didn't know why Scotty suddenly became so well-mannered. Perhaps her repeated pinchings had modified his behavior. Or maybe he'd had a religious experience.

Scotty didn't say what made him look forward to church. But it had become the easiest thing to wake him on Sunday mornings. On school days, Scotty lay virtually comatose. His sisters would poke and prod, yank the covers off him; once Maggie even poured a cup of water on his head.

But now on Sundays, he bolted out of bed, dressed himself, and sat waiting on the sofa, always the first one ready.

Claire told the Judge, "I think Scotty likes church."

. . .

The final Sunday in January, Scotty and a boy he didn't know played outside on the playground at St. Stephen's Episcopal Church. In minutes the service would begin. It was a snowless Sunday, and a crisp wind blew over the frozen playground. The boy complained that he wanted to go inside where it was warm.

"Stay out," Scotty demanded. He looked toward the entrance to the church parking lot. "It'll be worth it," he said. Minutes earlier Scotty had promised the boy that if he waited he would see something incredible.

The boy stuffed his hands deeper into his parka and said, "What are we waiting for?"

"You'll see."

The boy shivered as he and Scotty waited.

"There, I told you," Scotty finally said, pointing to a station wagon that turned into the church parking lot. Scotty pulled himself up onto the cold bars of the jungle gym. Then he hung upside down from the knees, locking his ankles together—and from this batlike vantage point, he watched as Tim Myerly's mom got out of the family car. He watched as she gathered her black shiny purse and wrapped a scarf around her neck and led her children into church. By this time the blood in Scotty's head had pumped downward, forcing veins to emerge. The boy waiting with Scotty said, "It looks like you got a road map running down your face." Scotty told him to be quiet.

The wooden fence surrounding the playground stood as high as Mrs. Myerly's neck; from Scotty's perspective, only her head could be seen moving.

He hung upside down so long that his face turned bright red and his eyes watered, causing Mrs. Myerly to blur.

After she had gone inside, Scotty used the boy to pull himself upright. And while the blood drained from his face, Scotty said, "Do you think she noticed me?"

The boy shrugged and mumbled. He didn't know.

Scotty hoped that she hadn't seen him, for he didn't want her to know that he was watching her. Then he dropped to the cold concrete of the playground and hurried after the Myerlys. If he moved fast enough, he could see where she hung her winter coat, so that then, after the service, he would know where to hide so he could study her every move.

(4)

In the endless white of the February snow, Scotty tried to step where no one had walked: He liked to turn around every thirty or forty steps and see the path he'd made, see his imprint. This meant a longer walk home from school and in more treacherous terrain.

Two girls ahead of him pretended to smoke, bringing an invisible cigarette to their mouths for a moment, then blowing out. Because of the cold air, steam came out of their mouths when they exhaled.

Scotty shook his head and thought, Stupids.

Tom Conway stood bundled up in front of Scotty's house. With his snot-wet scarf wrapped mummylike around his face, he appeared to have frozen while he waited for Scotty. "Want to see something?" Tom asked.

Scotty didn't want to see Tom's grenade again. So Scotty said, "No."

"You've never seen anything like this before."

"No."

"Chicken," Tom said. "You're Kitty Litter. You're a Q-tip."

Tom turned and headed toward his house. "You're a loser," Tom said under his breath.

Scotty surprised himself by following after.

Scotty and Tom stood on milk crates as Tom propped up the big white freezer lid in the Conways' garage.

"The springs are broken."

Tom wedged in a stick that helped keep the heavy lid lifted. The cold air pushed up and bathed the faces of the two boys.

"My dad is having us save her."

"Yeah?"

"For the fur."

"For the fur?"

"Yeah."

Tom struggled to remove a basket of frozen vegetables, a package of hamburger meat.

"There. She's down there."

Scotty looked past a box of Fudgsicles and a half-gallon container of Borden's ice cream.

"Where?"

Tom pointed to a package of white butcher paper securely wrapped.

"Oh man."

"Yep."

"How do I know?"

"Do you see Lassie anywhere?"

Scotty looked around. The Conways had kept their puppy in the garage. She slept in an old TV box. But the box was gone. The dog dish was gone. "So you see."

Tom poked at the package, exposing a tuft of dog fur.

"Now do you believe me?"

The Conways' collie had been crushed by Sergeant Conway's car when he drove into their garage late one night. The puppy crawled out into the snow-covered front yard, her back legs broken, and collapsed, dead. Sergeant Conway wrapped the animal up and placed it in the freezer, where it had spent the last several days. As he stared down at the frosted package, Scotty thought, Because they loved the dog.

But, in truth, the dog's being frozen had nothing to do with love.

"The fur is worth something," Tom told Scotty.

"Yeah?"

"Yeah, worth money. Lots of cashola."

"Yeah?"

"Worth more dead than alive."

"No."

"Yep."

Scotty suddenly felt sick.

"Oh yeah," Tom said, as if strangely pleased. "The dog is definitely worth more dead."

(5)

Occasionally the Judge attempted a new recipe. The night he tried to make a meat loaf it was burned severely. He set it on the table and the Ocean children stared at its charred remains.

"The inside is still good," the Judge said as he used a spatula to lift the meat loaf out of the bread pan. He cut off the ends. "See, the middle is fine. Eat up everybody."

"No thank you," said Claire.

"No thanks," said Maggie.

"This is not up for discussion, girls. This is the meal."

But the girls had no interest in even tasting it.

The Judge smiled tensely and said, "It's edible. More than edible. It's healthy. Eat around the burnt parts, all right?" Then he put a slice of meat loaf on each of their plates.

"Dad," Claire said, "drive us to McDonald's."

"Yeah, Dad," Maggie said.

"This is perfectly good!" the Judge shouted. "You're to eat what's served. I'm not a restaurant."

"That's good," Claire said, "because you'd have no customers."

"Scotty's eating it."

Scotty had taken a bite and tried not to make a face as he chewed.

"He hates it," Maggie said.

"You like it, don't you, Scotty?"

Scotty leaned over his plate and spit out the half-chewed meat loaf. He had tried but he couldn't swallow it.

"Aw, crap," the Judge said, scooping the rest of the meat

loaf up in his hands, moving to the back door, kicking it open with his foot. He heaved the burnt meat loaf like a football. It landed in the snow.

The Judge returned to his chair and ate in silence. None of the Ocean children moved. Each of them stared down at their plates. After the Judge finished eating, he wiped his mouth with his napkin and said, "None of you know how lucky you are. Do you? You have no idea."

The next night the Judge made spaghetti. Claire and Maggie both commented on how good it smelled. The Judge thanked them and announced he had come up with a new family activity. In an effort to make the family meal more pleasant, and to teach his children the importance of gratitude, the Judge instituted a predinner ritual. Before grace, and always going from youngest to oldest, each family member was to list what they were thankful for on that particular day.

Scotty paused the first time, because he wasn't good at this yet. Before the next several dinners he would stammer for a long time, and Maggie would sigh, Claire would press her mouth into a forced smile, and the Judge would wait patiently, because it was important to find something to be thankful for.

Scotty would say, "I'm thankful for the snow."

Maggie would grunt.

The Judge would say, "It's something."

And Scotty would repeat, "Yeah, it's something."

"And what else, Scotty, are you thankful for?"

And he would say, "My new tooth," or he'd mention a new toy. Once he was thankful for everything everyone else was thankful for.

Maggie's thank-yous were usually material—a lipstick, a

curling iron, or her new go-go boots. Claire's thank-yous were often of a political nature. "I'm thankful for the lives of the Kennedy brothers and Martin Luther King, Jr. I'm thankful I received my POW bracelet in the mail."

The Judge always looked each child in the eye and then said, "I'm thankful for my wonderful kids."

One night Scotty listed everything he could think up. "I'm thankful for corn muffins and . . . my new shoes and . . . and Tang breakfast drink . . . and that I'm not frozen in the freezer."

"Hear! Hear!" the Judge said. Word had spread around the neighborhood about the Conways' puppy.

"Anything else, Scotty?"

"Huh?"

"That you're thankful for?"

"Oh yeah. Sheila."

"Sheila?" the Judge asked. "Who is Sheila?"

Scotty wouldn't say.

Claire asked, "Does Scotty have a girlfriend?"

"No."

"Then who is Sheila?"

Later, as they did laundry, Claire asked Scotty to describe her. He did the best he could explaining her hair, her smile, the size of her eyes.

Claire poured in detergent. They were doing a load of whites. "What's Sheila's last name? If she's that pretty, you better tell me her name."

"No," Scotty said.

"Then I don't believe you."

"She's real."

"Let me see her."

"You've seen her and you don't even know it."

Tim Myerly's mom was named Sheila. Scotty had heard Mr. Myerly call her that the previous Sunday. "Sheila," he kept saying, "Sheila, it's time to go home."

If he were ever to speak with her, Scotty decided, he'd never call her Sheila—better to call her Tim's Mom. She'd like that, he thought. She'd smile.

Lately Scotty had been tagging along with Tim after Sunday services. Tim didn't trust Scotty because he appeared too friendly. But soon the boys were playing during every coffee hour. Sometimes Tim's younger brother, Jeff, who had just turned five but was taller than Scotty, played, too. Rounding out the Myerly family, there was the baby sister, six-month-old Elizabeth, and the father, a salesman for Massey-Ferguson tractors. But most important, there was Tim Myerly's mom, whose effortless smile made Scotty think he was one of her own.

While the adults socialized in the parish hall, Scotty would play hide-and-seek with the Myerly brothers. Whether he was hiding or whether he was "it," Scotty found a way to sneak downstairs to the nursery. There he would linger behind people and doors staring at Tim Myerly's mom, who always stood holding Elizabeth, talking with Mrs. Hargroves or Miss Jeannette Snead, in the center of the nursery.

Each week Scotty yearned for Mrs. Sheila Myerly to do one thing. He would wait. She never failed him. It always came after Sheila handed Elizabeth over to one of her women friends.

(Tim or Jeff might run past and she might say, "Boys, not so fast." She said it in such a way a boy would never want to run fast again.)

Scotty's favorite moment began as she opened her shiny black purse. Somehow she never searched or fumbled; she never removed anything extra. Without pause and without even the slightest glance down, she produced a long, white cigarette. The cigarette went to her lips. She reached in again and out came a silver lighter. She lit the cigarette, inhaled slowly, her cheeks sinking in. She looked up and exhaled her smoke in thin, perfect streams. A white cloud of smoke floated above her and Scotty wanted more than anything for it to blow his way.

(6)

On a Friday night in early February, ten of Maggie's closest friends came to the house for a birthday party sleep-over. The Judge made sloppy joes and Claire made a cake, and there were presents, but mainly the party consisted of girls staying up most of the night, wrapped in their sleeping bags, talking about girl matters.

In the morning Scotty found Maggie and her friends spread out in their sleeping bags, so he was forced to watch cartoons on the black-and-white TV in the Judge's room.

Later, when the girls finally woke up, the Judge made French toast, much of which he burned.

.   .   .

That Sunday a minor snowstorm almost ruined the second part
of Maggie's birthday weekend. Scotty, Maggie, and Claire had
been dropped off at the Des Moines Ice Arena, home of the
minor league hockey team, the Des Moines Capitals. On non-
game days, the arena was open to the public for ice skating.
And since Maggie had received a pair of perfectly sized white
skates from Joan in the mail, she was eager to try them out.

The Judge reminded them as they climbed out of the car
that Joan was driving the ninety miles from Iowa City, and
the snow would most likely delay her. If she hadn't arrived
by the end of the skating session, they were to call the Judge
and he would come get them.

Scotty stood near the concession stand peering over the ice
rink wall. He had no interest in skating himself, but he didn't
mind watching: He especially liked when people fell.

A pair of cold hands covered his eyes, and a familiar voice
said, "Guess who?" (Joan had arrived in time to catch the final
fifteen minutes of the afternoon skate.) He pulled her hands
away, turned, and saw her. She appeared clear-eyed, her cheeks
pink from the winter air, and she kissed him on the forehead,
making a loud smack. Then she scanned the ice rink looking
for the girls. She found Claire circling in the center of the ice.
Then, at the far end of the rink, where the opposition's goal
would be if it were a hockey game, she saw Maggie wobbling
along, her ankles turned in. Joan shouted and waved.

"Look at them," she told Scotty. "They're good."

"Yeah," Scotty said.

"Why aren't you skating?"

"It's stupid."

"Oh, well, that's all right."

Joan had been a cheerleader in college and anyone watching

would have seen a hint of the kind of cheerleader she had been: peppy, loud, animated. But the more vocal and more supportive Joan became, the more Scotty wanted to go home.

When the announcement came over the loudspeaker asking the skaters to clear the rink, those on the ice let out a collective moan. As the girls skated toward the exit door, Joan told them they could skate for another session if they wanted. "No," Maggie said, quickly unlacing and removing her skates. She already had the beginnings of a blister.

While Joan and the girls talked, Scotty watched as a special machine, resembling a street cleaner, drove out onto the rink. It sprayed water over the cut, gashed ice. This smoothed over the rough edges and made the surface look like the glaze on a doughnut.

After a brisk walk across the street to Shakey's Pizza, Joan and her children settled into a corner booth. Joan shared a pitcher of Pepsi with the girls. No beer, they would report later to the Judge, *no beer*. Scotty drank 7-UP. He studied the red-and-white-checkered tablecloth with its blotches of tomato paste and crumbs from previous pizza crusts.

Maggie asked if it was okay to order a Suicide pizza (which consisted of every topping Shakey's offered). Joan said, "It's your day, Maggie."

Trying to cram weeks of life into an hour of pizza and conversation proved not easy, as Maggie and Joan were both eager to talk. Maggie recounted her party. And Joan said she was glad it had gone well.

On a television that hung above the place where soda pop and beer were served, Scotty watched the opening moments of *Wide World of Sports* ("The thrill of victory, the agony of defeat!"). On the screen, a skier fell and flipped over and rolled and bounced and skidded for hundreds of yards. Every week he made the same fall. Scotty always wondered how badly the skier was hurt.

Joan spoke about how nice it was being back in school. She hinted that next time they got together, they could all study. She explained how she had given up art and felt great about it. She wanted to learn something useful. She wanted to help people. Claire told her mother that she was proud, and Maggie agreed. Joan described her apartment in Iowa City. "Barely enough room for me, but soon I will get a bigger place with a fold-out sofa. You all can come and visit."

Outside, the snow was accumulating on the street faster than the street plows could remove it.

Scotty said little during the eating of pizza. He didn't like pizza.

Maggie accused him of never trying it.

"Yes, I have."

Claire asked Scotty when he last had eaten it.

Scotty shrugged.

"Maybe you'll like it. It's a scientific fact that your taste buds change every twenty-one days."

"No way," Scotty said.

"It's true."

"No way!"

Apparently Claire had read an "Ask Andy" column in the paper that had explained all about taste buds. Children from all over America wrote Andy with their questions—Why does a butterfly have dots on its wings? What is a drone bee?—and each day Andy chose a winner question and answered it. The winner got a set of junior encyclopedias, and, best of all, his name and hometown printed in the paper.

"Andy said that taste buds change every twenty-one days."

Joan interrupted and said that Scotty didn't have to eat it if he didn't want to. She tried to order him a hamburger or fried chicken but Shakey's only served pizza. "Maybe," she said, "I can run you over to McDonald's."

Maggie interrupted, "No one is going anywhere. Scotty just wants attention."

A group of boys about Maggie's age came in from the cold. Soon after they sat down, several pizzas arrived for them. They had phoned ahead. The center pizza had twelve candles on it.

The entire restaurant joined in and sang "Happy Birthday."

Joan became distracted. She flagged down the waitress and whispered something in her ear.

"It's okay, Mom," Maggie said.

"No. No, it's not."

Scotty didn't know what Joan was planning, but the waitress appeared annoyed.

Joan said that she would order another pizza then, but it must have candles. She put her arm around Maggie, smiled to the waitress, and said, "She's eleven today."

The waitress said she would see what she could do and left.

"Mom, my birthday was Friday."

"I know. But she doesn't need to know that." Then Joan looked suddenly sad. "I didn't know they did such things here."

"It's really okay," Claire said. "Maggie already had a party. She had cake and candles, she had everything."

Joan said for her kids not to worry. Turning to Scotty, and perhaps to change the subject altogether, she said, "Scotty, you seem different."

"Yeah, he's different all right," Maggie told Joan. "Look at his teeth."

Scotty had a couple of permanent teeth that had grown in. The Judge called them man-sized teeth in a boy-sized mouth. According to Maggie, they looked like big poster boards, and she had threatened to paint messages on them: No Parking or Child Crossing. "Or maybe," she said, "I'll write a report on them and bring you to school for Mrs. Mendenhall to grade.

Joan said, "It's not his teeth that I was thinking of." Then she squeezed his knee under the table. Scotty said, "Ow."

While waiting for the birthday pizza, Joan began to run out of things to talk about. She gave Maggie a handful of quarters with the order that she play whatever she wanted on the juke-box. "Dizzy" and "Crystal Blue Persuasion" and "I Can't Get Next to You" were her first three choices.

While Joan tried to get the waitress's attention, Claire sent Scotty to see if the Judge had arrived. Scotty opened the door and saw the Dodge Dart idling, snowflakes swirling around the headlights, the wipers batting away the flakes at the moment they hit the windshield.

Back at the booth, Joan was arguing with the waitress: "It's just a simple pizza with candles. It shouldn't take that long."

Scotty said excitedly, "He's here!"

"Already?" Joan said.

She watched as her children put on their coats and mittens. Claire explained that they didn't want to keep their dad waiting.

(7)

February was a busy month at Clover Hills Elementary. Mrs. Mansfield's fourth grade class built a miniature volcano out of papier-mâché and chicken wire. The multipurpose room was filled with second, third, and fourth graders, and Keith Hoyt and Bob Fowler, big, lumpy boys who lived near Scotty, gave a speech about the nature of volcanos, how they are formed, how they can erupt at any time.

Scotty found this interesting.

Mrs. Mansfield lit the match for them that caused their miniature volcano to belch; then a black, fizzy lavalike foam poured out. For fifteen seconds nothing had been so magnificent, but then it was over and Mrs. Boyden and the other teachers were nudging their students to stand and march single file back to their respective classrooms.

In Scotty's class Mrs. Boyden began to introduce the concept of fractions. She had many drawings of sliced-up pies to help illustrate.

That Friday, Leann Callahan's father (who delivered milk for Anderson Erickson Dairy) came to school. He poured milk and other ingredients into a glass bottle. Scotty and his classmates took turns shaking it, and soon the contents had solidified. "I made butter," Scotty would later brag to the Judge.

Because of below-freezing temperatures and the occasional snowfall, PE was always indoors and consisted primarily of games of dodge ball in the multipurpose room. Scotty excelled at dodge ball.

In Art class, the students brought empty cereal boxes, which they began to decorate with red, pink, and white construction paper. Using scissors, they cut paper hearts of varying sizes and pasted them on. The Valentine boxes were hung in anticipation of February 14. Mrs. Boyden sent a note home with each student explaining that Valentines were to be distributed on the twelfth, as the fourteenth was a Sunday. She also suggested that minimal candy should be given as gifts. During rest time, when the students closed their eyes and laid their heads down on their desks, she moved about the room, leaving a candy heart on each desk. Each heart had a message stamped on it. Scotty's was "Be Mine."

Mrs. Burns, the music teacher, wheeled her metal cart full of instruments (rhythm stick, drums, bells) into Mrs. Boyden's classroom. She had done this twice a week since the New Year. And for most of February, she would teach the students patriotic songs.

"Boys and girls, why do we honor Abraham Lincoln?"

No hands went into the air.

Mrs. Burns continued, "Abraham Lincoln freed the slaves and saved the country and if he hadn't, we wouldn't be Americans."

Big whoop, Scotty thought.

"Today we will sing patriotic songs. As a way of saying thank you to Abraham Lincoln, whose birthday is today." Then Mrs. Burns led the class in singing "The Star-Spangled Banner," "Yankee Doodle Dandy," and, finally, "America the Beautiful."

She had a technique where she would sing a phrase and then her students would repeat. That was the way to learn. So when she sang "Oh beautiful for spacious skies," the kids dutifully repeated.

"For amber waves of grain." This, too, they echoed.

"For purple mountain majesties . . ."

Scotty stopped. He looked over to where Carole was sitting. She had continued to sing with the others. Had she forgotten her painting? He felt heat in his face as he yelled to her, but the singing drowned out his shouts. And by the time the room quieted, Scotty had darted down the aisle and out of the classroom. With her face in the songbook, Mrs. Burns saw only a blur run past. She walked quickly to the door and looked down the hall where she saw Scotty Ocean run past the first grade classrooms, past kindergarten, past the principal's office, and turn toward the teachers' lounge.

When he pushed open the door, Scotty entered a cloud of smoke. Several teachers sat with cigarettes—Mrs. Mansfield of fourth grade, Mrs. Pfeifer of fifth, and Mr. Shelton, the PE teacher, all turned toward Scotty and glared.

Mrs. Boyden stubbed out her cigarette with great force, started to speak when Scotty Ocean stuck out his arm. "Be quiet," he seemed to say. Mrs. Boyden exhaled and Scotty fought coughing. She spoke with impatience. "You're not allowed in here . . ."

But with his voice, high in pitch, Scotty Ocean interrupted. He said two words, and two words only.

Mrs. Boyden reached for Scotty. He spoke again, this time with fuller voice. He spoke the same two words.

She got hold of his arm, pinched his skin, but he struggled free and took to the halls of Clover Hills Elementary. Mr. Shelton, the PE teacher, took after him. But Scotty Ocean was not to be stopped. He shouted, "Purple mountains! Purple mountains! Purple mountains!"

. . .

The next day when Scotty entered the classroom, the seating arrangement had been changed. The desks had been placed in a giant U. Scotty's desk was now closest to Mrs. Boyden, and the whole first day of the new seating arrangement Scotty sat wishing the desks could move back to their original positions. He loved his old spot, watching the day's proceedings as if they were the television, but now—with the dubious placement of his desk practically flush against Mrs. Boyden's, he was the featured attraction.

For a few days Scotty would be the talk of the second grade.

(8)

Everybody behaved well for Mrs. Boyden the day Bev Fowler returned to class. No one talked out of turn and the moment of silence after the Pledge of Allegiance seemed particularly long. Even Bev did not know how popular she was about to become.

The week before, Bev Fowler's mom had died in the parking lot of Dahl's grocery store.

Carole Staley told a group of boys including Scotty that Bev had been sent in to buy a package of hamburger buns. When she came out of Dahl's, she found her mother slumped over the steering wheel, the car horn blaring. "She pulled her mother off the wheel and felt the limpness."

No one moved as Carole told the sequence of events.

That night, during dinner, the Judge explained the medical reasons. "Some people," he said, "a very small number of people, have what's called an aneurysm. Doctors have no way of knowing if a person has one. Some aneurysms, such as Mrs. Fowler's, are on the brain." And then he said, as if it were good news, "She died instantly. No pain. No warning, of course, but at least there was no pain."

None of the children was eating. Appetites had been lost.

"But you must understand—aneurysms are very rare." The Judge used a toothpick to dislodge a chunk of meat from between his teeth. "If I was a betting man, I'd put my money that none of you would have an aneurysm." His children still didn't move. Finally the Judge said, "Maggie, could you pass the salt."

On Bev's second day back, Scotty studied her from ten feet. He stood by the textured globe. (It was too cold to play outside, so recess was indoors.) Bev watched Ruth Rethman and Leann Callahan play ticktacktoe. Bev crossed one leg over the other as she stood. She had yet to smile.

"She touched her dead mother," Tom Conway whispered.

"Yeah," said Scotty.

"We know someone who touched a dead person."

"Yeah," said Scotty again, forgetting for a moment that Tom Conway's family kept a dead puppy frozen in their freezer.

Scotty envied Bev Fowler. His mother had only left, and leaving did not pull the same weight as dying.

That night before sleep, he imagined Joan's death. It would have to be worse than Mrs. Fowler's. Anything less would be a letdown for his friends. Anything less and they'd say, "Too bad but look at what Bev Fowler had to go through."

(9)

On television, many of the mothers on Scotty's favorite shows were dead.

On *My Three Sons,* Chip and Ernie had no mother. They had Uncle Charlie, of course, who did many of the motherly chores. And even though Fred MacMurray was dating Ernie's teacher (they would marry that March), she would never be a real mother.

On *The Courtship of Eddie's Father,* Eddie had no mother. He had Mrs. Livingston, a Korean maid, and his father, a funny and kind and kite-flying father.

On *Family Affair,* Buffy and Jody had Uncle Bill and Mr. French—no mother, though.

Bonanza was the most motherless of shows. In fact, all three of Ben Cartwright's boys had different mothers, all dead. But they had Hop Sing, their trusted Chinese cook.

TV provided the necessary evidence. Not only was it possible to survive without a mother; it seemed to improve your chances of having your own TV show.

Scotty wanted to tell Bev Fowler what he had figured out. Maybe it would make her smile or at least feel not so bad. But Bev always had her many friends around her, and he could never get close enough.

"School is canceled," the Judge told his children. "You're snowed out."

The Judge drove the Dodge through the storm. His snow tires helped him handle rough roads. He had mounds of paperwork to sort through at the courthouse. Claire was put in charge, and in her usual crack-the-whip style, she had both Maggie and Scotty shoveling immediately after *Captain Kangaroo*. The snow was heavy and wet. Scotty worked on the sidewalk and cut a path. Maggie and Claire only did one half of the driveway because only one car would be coming and going.

The afternoon was given over to building snowmen and snow forts.

Later in the day, while outside, Scotty broke off a small tree branch, and when he saw a row of jagged icicles hanging from a neighbor's gutter, he ran the stick along breaking each at its base, causing missiles of ice to pierce the snow below. He took the largest icicle and licked it like an ice cream bar. He walked nonchalantly with it in one hand. Finally, Scotty had a weapon, and even grenade-toting Tom Conway (who was carving out a fort in a drift on the side of his house) knew to keep his distance.

The Crows had a Toro snowblower and Andrew was allowed to operate it. Their driveway and sidewalks were spotless, reminding Scotty of the snow cleaner that the Cat in the Hat used.

A snowball hurtled through the air just missing Scotty's head. It splattered on the garage door.

Andrew stood in his snowsuit. Bright orange stripes of reflector tape were sewn onto the legs and arms so that at night he would glow.

Scotty hurried inside.

That night as the family watched TV, the doorbell rang. Scotty opened the door and felt the cold from winter squeezing past the storm door. He rubbed an eye opening in the frosted glass and peeking out saw Andrew Crow standing on the porch.

"I've come to collect," Andrew shouted.

Andrew Crow had become the paper boy for the neighborhood, delivering the *Des Moines Register* six mornings a week, Monday through Saturday.

His cheeks red and eyes glazed from the cold, he stood hoping Scotty would ask him in.

But Scotty didn't. Instead he disappeared from view and ran circles around the coffee table, shouting, "It's him! It's him!"

Claire got up from the sofa where she had been stretched out, poked her head around the corner, and, upon seeing Andrew Crow, made a gagging sound.

The Judge gave Scotty the amount owed in exact change. And Scotty returned to the vestibule. "There you go," Scotty said, dropping the last coin into Andrew's glove.

And Andrew looked up at Scotty and had an idea.

Andrew Crow waited outside while Scotty asked the Judge. The Judge told Scotty to show Andrew inside. The Judge sat on the living room sofa, a large bowl of popcorn sitting in his lap. *Mannix* blared on the TV.

"Hello, Andrew," the Judge said.

"Hello, sir."

"Scotty tells me you want to hire him to help you."

Andrew had never thought about hiring. He wondered if Scotty might like to tag along. It would be fun to have someone to talk to.

"Scotty's curious about what his wages will be."

Scotty stopped breathing. He wasn't curious. He didn't care about wages.

Andrew had never considered paying Scotty. He saw giving him the opportunity to help him, if anything, to be a privilege, and certainly not a job.

But the Judge was firm and Andrew quickly agreed to seventy-five cents for helping. His first offer had been a quarter but the Judge said a quarter was out of the question.

Scotty couldn't believe it. Not only would he get to hang out with Andrew; he would get to walk around the streets when everybody was asleep, and he would be making money, too.

Life had a way of surprising.

(11)

"Maggie? Is that you, Maggie?"

Scotty wondered, When would his voice change? When would he sound like a man?

"Claire?"

Scotty held the receiver and spoke in his lowest voice. "No, it's Scotty."

"Oh," she said. "Hello, little love."

He knew his mother's voice. And he knew she was forcing the happy tone on the phone.

"Scotty, you there?"

Scotty mumbled something in response.

"What was that, sweetheart?"

He said nothing. He could hear her inhale on a cigarette. After a silence, Joan asked for Scotty to call the Judge to the phone.

"He's not home."

"What was that, honey?"

"He's not *home*."

"Of course he is—"

"No."

The Judge had taken Maggie to dance class and dropped Claire off at the library.

"He left you at home all by yourself?"

"Yes."

"Oh."

"I'm seven, Mom. Seven can handle this."

"Of course."

He was right, seven could. For seven handled helping with the laundry. Seven handled matching socks and shining the Judge's shoes and dressing himself every morning. Seven managed.

"Could you write your father a note?"

Scotty mumbled an "Okay."

"Get paper and pencil."

Scotty set the phone down and pulled open drawer after drawer. He easily found a small pad of paper, but no pencil or pen.

"No pencil."

"Scotty, hurry please."

"But there's no pencil."

"Hurry."

He searched the bookshelf. He climbed the stairs checking each step; he ran to his room where he found crayons.

"I got a crayon," he said speaking into the upstairs phone. "Here's my message."

Joan started to speak when Scotty realized he'd left the pad of paper downstairs. He dropped the phone and ran down the steps, turned the corner and picked up the kitchen phone as Joan finished giving her message.

"What did you say?"

"Scotty," she sighed.

"One more time."

"Write: Mother . . . is . . . in . . ."

Scotty prided himself at being fast in many areas, but his penmanship took an eternity. Joan would have to wait.

"Where are you, honey?"

"At my house. Kitchen."

"No, honey, where are you with the writing?"

"I'm on 'is.' "

"Tell him I'm in . . ."

Joan Ocean began to sob.

Scotty waited to hear the next word to write. He didn't want to seem pushy so as she wept on the other end, he went back and crossed the "t" in "Mother." Then he tried to imagine what the next word would be. Mother is in . . .

Scotty heard his mother say, "One moment, please. Just one more moment."

"What, Mom?"

"I'm talking to someone else, honey. Just hold on."

She must have covered the receiver, he decided, because he could only hear muffled voices. When she spoke to him again, her voice had no feeling. It made Scotty think she was talking to someone else.

"Tell your dad—tell him I'm in jail."

Joan said good-bye. Scotty said nothing as the phone went dead, then a dial tone. Scotty was pleased because jail was a word he knew how to spell. He wrote it in big letters with his blue crayon.

He left the note on the kitchen table and went into the living room where a plate full of his toast crusts waited. He flipped the channels in hopes of finding the Salem girl or the Purina chuck wagon.

Later he went upstairs where he found the phone he had forgotten to hang up. When he got close, he heard the throbbing cry a phone makes when off the hook. It was as if it were calling him. "Scotty," it said. "Scotty, Scotty."

As soon as he got home, the Judge called the police in Iowa City. Joan had crashed her car into a telephone pole. She had cut her forehead, received stitches: She had been drinking. The car was damaged, not totaled, and she'd be able to drive it. After being treated at a hospital, she was taken to the Iowa City County Jail where she was to spend the night.

The Judge told his worried children all that he thought they should know. Scotty didn't hear much of what he said—only the good news that his mother was a criminal.

At school, Scotty expected and got a small crowd of boys who wanted to know all the details.

Tom Conway asked Scotty, "Will she get the death penalty?"

"Maybe."

"What's she in for?"

"Lots of things," Scotty told the boys.

"I believe in the death penalty," Chip Fisher said. His father was a policeman.

"Me, too," Scotty said.

"Even if it's your mother?"

"For what she did, yep."

"What'd she do? Murder somebody?"

"Maybe," Scotty said.

"No. We woulda heard 'bout it."

"You gotta kill to get the death penalty."

"Scotty's a liar. He lies."

Scotty shrugged. They all had boring mothers—mothers who baked, mothers who sewed, mothers who drove station wagons. His mother was a criminal.

Mrs. Boyden rang the bell signaling the end of recess.

"You don't mean the death penalty part."

"I do."

Mrs. Boyden rang the recess bell a second time and the others sprinted toward the classroom. Scotty walked, taking his own sweet time. He knew those who weren't looking at him were thinking about him, his mother and her crime, and how great it must be to be Scotty Ocean.

Within minutes, as Mrs. Boyden flashed addition and subtraction cards, Bev Fowler put her head down on the table and began to cry uncontrollably. Mrs. Boyden took Bev by the hand and led her out of the classroom as the others watched silently.

After a short time, Mrs. Boyden opened the classroom door and said, "Scott, could you come here please?"

Outside, Bev's shoulders heaved up and down, her eyes all pink and wet.

"Tell Beverly the truth."

Scotty looked at her as if he had no idea what she meant.

"Your mother isn't going to be executed," she said as she squeezed Scotty's arm. "Tell her!"

Scotty turned to Mrs. Boyden, pressed his big front teeth into his bottom lip and glared. She said, without thought, "I'll get the principal."

Scotty said nothing to Bev Fowler, who continued crying with her hands brought up to cover her face. Scotty looked out to where the playground equipment stood. He heard the click of Mrs. Boyden's heels walking away. The click grew softer. It stopped when she turned into the carpeted office. Mr. Sheil, the principal, would be coming out soon, the weight of his body leaning forward, his bald head reflecting the fluorescent light.

While waiting outside the principal's office, Scotty watched the other children as they left for the day. Some kids carried home their art projects, and other kids lined up for the water fountain. Tim Myerly hurried past. Somewhere out in the parking lot, inside a station wagon, Mrs. Myerly waited.

The Judge had been contacted. He drove straight from the courthouse, and he was, as Maggie would say, steaming mad. He had gone immediately into the principal's office, where he met privately with Principal Sheil and Mrs. Boyden for over thirty minutes.

Scotty wondered what they were talking about.

Scotty knew he was in trouble, but he didn't seem to care.

When the Judge emerged from the office, he didn't look at Scotty. He said tersely, "Get your coat." Scotty did. "Get your things." Scotty had his lunch pail, his stocking cap, his mittens. "I have them."

"Let's go," the Judge said.

. . .

The Judge unlocked the car door with his key.

"Scotty, this is unacceptable. Do you know that?"

"Yes."

"You don't want me to have to come back to school. You know that, don't you?"

"I know," Scotty said as he climbed in the car.

"Because," the Judge said with utter certainty, "the next time I get called back, it won't be pretty."

(12)

That Sunday, Sheila Myerly came to church alone. No Tim or Jeff, no Elizabeth. No husband. It was just Sheila. And Scotty knew it was his chance.

He kept turning around and looking at her during the service. Maybe her children and her husband got burned up in a fire or crushed by a bus.

At the coffee hour, he watched from behind the glass door outside the nursery. It would be time to go home soon. He waited for her to take a cigarette. As everyone said their goodbyes, Sheila stood in her regular spot.

Finally, she reached into her purse and pulled out her weekly cigarette. She lit it.

"Tim's Mom?"

Sheila turned and looked down. Staring up at her was Scotty—his odd face with a lopsided smile and hair she longed to comb.

"Tim's Mom?"

"Yes, what is it?"

"Uhm. Uhm." His knees felt like liquid; his stomach contracted into a tight knot. "Uhm."

Sheila Myerly smiled at Scotty. This gave him the needed strength.

"Where's Tim?"

"The kids and their father went to Kansas City on a special trip."

"Oh."

Scotty stood for a moment. He didn't know what to do. Mrs. Sheila Myerly's ashes turned orange as she inhaled. The smoke poured out her mouth and Scotty closed his eyes, hoping the smoke would surround him. It floated above, at first, and he watched as it slowly began to descend.

Standing in Sheila Myerly's smoke, Scotty was transported. He wondered, Is this sex?

Mrs. Sheila Myerly giggled.

Scotty opened his eyes.

"I'll tell Tim you asked about him."

"Okay," Scotty said, turning, and then he stole away.

"And Scotty?"

"Yes?"

"Maybe sometime you'd like to spend the night at our house. Would you like that?"

"Huh?"

"An overnight. You come to our house. Spend the night."

Scotty wanted to celebrate, do something, dance, but he cocked his head, as if considering, and said, "I'll have to ask my dad."

(13)

That week on *Family Affair,* Buffy lost her doll Mrs. Beasley. Uncle Bill spent the entire show trying to find Mrs. Beasley. Through persistence and a bit of good luck, he found the doll in the trash receptacle and just in time, too, for the show was almost over for the week. He woke Buffy, who was missing both front teeth—she's only six, Scotty said to his sisters and the Judge—and she told Uncle Bill that she had been dreaming that he had found Mrs. Beasley. Then Uncle Bill held out Mrs. Beasley for Buffy and said, "Sometimes dreams come true."

(14)

"Wait till the car stops moving," the Judge shouted.

But Scotty had already swung open the car door. The Judge was about to yell at Scotty when he realized Sheila Myerly was approaching the car. She wore a wool sweater and matching earmuffs.

"We're so pleased Scotty could be with us," she told the Judge.

"He's been looking forward to this. Scotty, zip up your coat."

But Scotty wasn't listening. He grabbed his overnight bag, said, "Bye, Dad."

"And Scotty, remember what I told you."

Scotty hadn't listened at all during the drive across town. The Judge went over the proper behavior for an overnight guest. Scotty had never slept over anywhere before, and the Judge expected the typical first-night-away-from-home jitters. Claire and Maggie both cried at some point during their first overnights and called home. The Judge assumed Scotty would do the same.

That night, the Judge watched television while Claire did homework and Maggie painted her finger nails a bright pink. The Judge expected the phone to ring with Scotty on the other line, sobbing, wanting to come home, missing him.

But that call never came.

The Myerlys lived in a single-story house on Hillside Avenue, on the other side of the elementary school. Because of his work, Mr. Myerly often traveled, even on weekends. That weekend he was in Omaha at a convention.

"It's so good," Sheila Myerly said as Scotty stepped inside, "to have another man in the house."

Sheila Myerly had planned a whole series of games and activities.

That afternoon Scotty attended his first play. At the Des Moines Community Playhouse, Mrs. Myerly sat between her boys: Scotty sat next to Tim. Scotty's favorite part of the play was when an igloo descended on wires, and a woman in a bear suit kept talking about how cold she was. She got the audience to say "Brrrr" with her, and Scotty thought that was funny, how she talked to them and how she made them talk.

After the play, she drove the boys to McDonald's for dinner, dessert at Baskin-Robbins, then a night spent playing

games in their basement. The boys followed carefully constructed clues, which led to a plastic treasure chest filled with
gold-wrapped milk chocolate coins hidden under the basement
stairs. Also Sheila Myerly got down on her knees and played a
game of Nerf basketball. She and Scotty were a team. They
lost, but losing had never seemed so nice.

Later, while Tim, Jeff, and Scotty made various faces with
a Mr. Potato Head, Scotty took a break, went upstairs, and
wandered the house looking for the bathroom. He spied Mrs.
Myerly in the kitchen, her shirt lifted, her baby Elizabeth in
her arms.

She noticed Scotty and said, "What do you need, Scotty?"

He shrugged, then mumbled, "Bathroom."

"Oh. Down the hall, to the right."

Scotty didn't move. He said, "Tim's Mom?"

"Yes?"

"What are you doing?"

"I'm feeding my baby."

"Oh."

"There's milk in my breasts. And Elizabeth is drinking the
milk."

"Milk?"

"Yes."

"Oh."

"Your mother did the same for you."

"No."

"I'm sure she did."

"No."

Tim's mom held baby Elizabeth up in the air, patted lightly
on the baby's back. Then Mrs. Sheila Myerly looked up at
Scotty. "You better get ready for bed."

And Scotty did as she said.

. . .

The trundle bed pulled out from under the bottom bunk. Scotty was to sleep next to Jeff, while Tim Myerly had the top bunk. When Mrs. Myerly tucked in the boys, she gave them each a kiss on the cheek. Scotty got an identical kiss. She looked back at them and, as she turned off the light, said, "Sleep tight."

But Scotty couldn't sleep. Across the boys' bedroom, a night-light glowed. The night-light was the face of a clown, and it was close enough to the bedroom door that it could guide Scotty. In the hall, another night-light—clownless—showed Scotty the way.

Mrs. Myerly's bedroom door was open and the room was mostly dark except for moonlight, which streamed in through lace curtains, casting snowflakes of light.

Scotty could see her shape lying in the bed, the covers barely disturbed, for Mrs. Myerly was small and thin, and it appeared as if she'd barely lifted the covers and slid under them.

For a long time Scotty stood staring at her. He held out his arms and studied the patterns of light on his skin. He curled up on her bedroom carpet and fell asleep.

Sometime during his sleep, he crawled under Mrs. Myerly's quilt and wiggled his way close to her. He found her hands, and under the covers, kissed her fingers and the inside of her wrist. His little lips moved up her arm, past her elbow until he felt the chiffon of her nightgown.

"Who is under there?"

Scotty knew it was time to give himself away.

"Tim? Jeff?"

Scotty imagined the surprise. He threw off the covers, sat up on his knees, and went, "Boo."

Scotty couldn't make out her complete expression, but her voice—the tone—was firm and tight.

"Scotty, you shouldn't be here."

He was confused. She didn't seem like the same person who a few hours earlier had kissed him on the cheek.

At breakfast, Mrs. Myerly still wasn't her usual self.

Scotty used his fork to pick at his sunny-side up egg. The yoke split in two and he watched as the egg ran toward his toast. "No," Scotty said, as if trying to tell the egg to turn back.

"Just eat it," Mrs. Myerly said.

That Saturday morning, Claire and Maggie were surprised to see Scotty walk in the door. They had enjoyed the quiet while he'd been away.

"You're back early," Claire said from the sofa.

Scotty dropped his bag on the floor in the hallway.

Maggie, who was stretched out on the carpet, said, "Did you do something wrong?"

Scotty didn't answer, but he was beginning to realize he had.

(15)

The last snowfall of the year came in late March, the day before Easter, and that was the one and only time Scotty helped

Andrew on his paper route. Encompassing Pleasant Street, Center Street, Twenty-first Street, Twentieth Place, Twentieth Street, and Nineteenth Street, the route consisted of sixty-one houses. And Scotty, dressed in three layers of clothing, barely able to move, went along with Andrew Crow.

Because of the early hour, the Judge followed in the Dodge at a safe distance. Claire had insisted the Judge go along. "Scotty is too young to be out at that hour," she argued. And while she didn't say it, Claire didn't trust Andrew Crow.

The Judge knew she was right: It was too early for a seven-year-old.

"Do the first three houses. Skip the next two; do the last one," Andrew had said only minutes earlier.

With four papers, Scotty ran as fast as he could. He opened the screen door of the first house and folded the paper as Andrew had instructed, dividing it into thirds, then tucking one end inside the other. Andrew Crow could fold the papers as he walked. But Scotty had to set the other papers down, kneel, and struggle to get the paper to Andrew's specifications.

"It took me a while to get the hang of it," Andrew would later say. "And I'm in the seventh grade."

When Scotty got the paper folded in the best manner he could (after repeated tries), he walked up to the house, but the paper slipped from under his arm and fell onto the snow-covered porch. When it landed, the paper flopped open.

Scotty turned to see if Andrew had noticed but he'd already gone on to the next block.

It was dark and cold; snow covered every yard. While he stood motionless in his boots, his breathing became pained, his little shoulders rising and falling, Scotty called out, "Andrew? Andrew?"

A breeze blew through the ice-covered trees, and Scotty hurried to the next house. When he saw the name on the mailbox, he suddenly stopped. It said Fowler. The Fowler house. Inside the Fowler family was sleeping, dreaming. Maybe Bev was dreaming about Mrs. Fowler.

It would be impossible to explain later what he felt then, but standing in front of him—seeing her without seeing her—near an evergreen tree, Scotty felt her, Mrs. Fowler, whom he could remember only vaguely (except for her thick glasses, she was a blur in his memory)—Bev Fowler's dead mom stood before him.

"Hello, Scotty," he thought she said.

The Judge's car with its headlights on was idling at the bottom of the hill. Scotty didn't have far to run, but he couldn't move.

Bev Fowler's mom swayed in the wind the way the trees and bushes swayed.

Gusts of wind snapped his face in bursts. Scotty couldn't keep the warm tears from escaping—they rolled partway down his cheek. They rolled until they froze.

He listened as she spoke to him. Then he ran, almost falling, down the hill toward the Judge's car. He was out of breath when he opened the passenger door. He tried to talk. He moved his hands, talking with them, making jerky gestures, as he struggled to describe what he had seen.

"You saw what . . . her ghost?"

Scotty didn't know, but yes, he thought he had.

"Well, Scotty," the Judge said. "Not many people see ghosts."

Scotty spoke quickly, breathing in the middle of thoughts,

rushing to say it all. He told of how Mrs. Fowler was standing in front of the Fowler house, as if protecting it.

"What did she tell you?"

"She's watching. Keeping guard. Making sure that her family is safe."

Scotty finished his report, and in finishing, he had to sit through a long silence from the Judge. The silence gave Scotty the time to panic with this thought: Surely his father would yell at him, or, worse, laugh. Scotty had left himself wide open. He had lied about the death penalty, he'd disrupted school, he couldn't even tie his shoes. Having destroyed all credibility, he would certainly be sent to where the kids with giant heads filled with water lie around all the time.

And in that moment, as Scotty clenched his teeth and his heart punched against his ribs, the Judge said simply, "That sounds like something Mrs. Fowler would do."

Andrew appeared in the glare of the headlights. Rolling down the side window, the Judge explained that Scotty was too young to be a paper boy, so he was taking him home. And anticipating the next question, he said, "And yes, Andrew, you can keep your seventy-five cents."

Then the Judge drove Scotty home.

The following morning Scotty woke to find a basket full of chocolate eggs, jelly beans, speckled malted milk balls, and a chocolate bunny with a red bow.

He brought the Easter basket to his bed, dug around in the green plastic grass, and by breakfast he'd eaten half of his candy.

At church, the Oceans took their regular place.

Behind them, a few rows back, Mrs. Myerly sat between her two boys. She had an Easter lily pinned to her pink dress.

Scotty turned and waited for her to make eye contact, but she stayed focused on the minister. Scotty even waved.

"Scotty," Claire whispered, "behave."

He turned around, faced front, and thought, I guess she didn't see me.

THE WRONG CROWD

(1)

In the first days of spring, Scotty Ocean abandoned his quest
for another mother. Not because he didn't want one, but by
mid-April, he had a more pressing concern.

The group of fourth grade boys, the same ones who built
the volcano out of chicken wire, set their sights on Scotty the
April day he drank, in their opinion, too much water from the
water fountain as they waited in line.

They told him they would be waiting for him after school.

In Mrs. Boyden's classroom, while he sat dreading the end
of the school day, Scotty looked around at the kids in his class.
He had never felt so unpopular. He had a sometime friend in
Tom Conway, but even Carole Staley had turned her atten-
tions elsewhere, having taken a fancy to Craig Hunt and the
new way he combed his hair (a part in the middle).

.   .   .

That day he walked home with Maggie, who stayed two steps ahead of him. She liked the distance between them. It served her, because she didn't want anyone to think she was talking to her brother, especially the group of fourth grade boys who stood with their bikes just outside the Clover Hills Elementary entrance.

Scotty didn't look at any of them. He stayed as close to Maggie as he could get, walking with his head down. He tried to appear unafraid by concentrating on avoiding the cracks in the sidewalk.

Occasionally one of the boys would pedal up to where Scotty was walking behind Maggie, suddenly slam on his breaks, leaving a fishtail skid mark on the street. Mostly they kept their distance. Maggie Ocean was a popular girl. And as long as Scotty stayed near her, he would not be hurt.

While walking, Maggie gave Scotty a pep talk. She shared her own personal experience. "You can't figure out popularity," she said. She told of a girl in the fifth grade who had been the teacher's favorite in third. "In third grade everybody liked her."

Scotty asked, "Who?"

Maggie said, "Jodi Jerard."

Scotty went, "She's a dud."

"So you see my point."

Scotty nodded even though he wasn't putting it together. All he knew was Jodi Jerard was more of a dud than he was. He looked back to where the fourth grade boys—Cam Sweney, Bob Fowler (Bev's brother), and others circled on their bikes. He wondered if Maggie knew they were being followed.

Maggie was aware of them, but she thought they were trailing her. She continued with her popularity theories explaining how she, too, *once upon a time* had been unpopular. "Jodi Jerard had third grade and look where she is now. Fourth grade was more Becky Elder and Leann Stonebrook. Fifth grade is mine." Maggie Ocean ruled fifth grade.

Scotty shrugged. He only understood what was being said in terms of him. And it wasn't so much *what* was being said but rather the tone *in which* it was said. Maggie's tone had a conflicted quality. Most of her sounded comforting but there was a warble, a kind of raspy bite to her voice that seemed to say, "I love watching you suffer, Scotty Ocean."

As they walked, Scotty ran a stick along the Orvises' white picket fence. He stopped listening to his sister and started listening to himself. Scotty felt loved and despised at the same time. The disparity of such feelings did not trouble him, for that is how he usually felt. And even though his television heroes—Jody on *Family Affair,* Little Joe on *Bonanza,* and Ernie on *My Three Sons*—seemed to escape such mixed-up emotions, they did have troubles of their own. Jody broke a vase once, Ernie lost his glasses, and that Sunday night, Scotty watched as Little Joe's heart broke when the woman he loved turned out to be a liar, a cheat. Little Joe felt like crying but he didn't cry because he's not a crier. And when Little Joe gets sad, Scotty noted, he climbs on his horse and rides into town or sits at home at the Ponderosa and eats a good meal, and waits for everything to work out, which for Little Joe Cartwright, it always did.

"So Scotty," Maggie concluded as they stepped up onto the porch of their house. "What do you think?"

"Uhm."

"You didn't listen, did you?"

"Yeah, I . . ."

"I just told you the secret of being popular. And you didn't listen." Maggie let the screen door slam. "Do you know how many people want to know the secret of being popular?"

Scotty stood on the porch for a moment, then looked back up the street two houses to where the pack of fourth grade boys stood, straddling their bikes. He had survived the day.

(2)

April birthdays included Mrs. Boyden, who asked the kids to sing "Happy Birthday" to her, which they did. She wouldn't reveal her age, but she said that it was her greatest hope that all of the students would live as long as she had. "May you be so lucky."

Ruth Rethman, whose actual birthday wasn't until the end of June, had elected to celebrate hers on April 23.

Years earlier, Mrs. Boyden had realized there was an injustice being done to the students with summer birthdays. Since school would not be in session, she thought it only fair to let each kid with a summer birthday designate a day as theirs.

In the weeks to come, Shari Tussey and the Hammer twins would have their own parties, which weren't parties really, but opportunities for mothers or fathers to bring treats for the entire class and for the honored student to wear the cone-shaped birthday hat for the entire day.

"Scotty," Mrs. Boyden said, "you need to pick a date for your party."

"No."

"Don't you want a party?"

Scotty shook his head.

Mrs. Boyden had never had a student who didn't want a party. "Of course you do. Everyone wants a party."

"No," Scotty said as he wandered out to recess. Anyway, he thought, doesn't she get it? I'm not turning eight.

(3)

Scotty's alliance with Tom Conway was made out of necessity.

Tom had gone through an unpopular phase early in the year. He'd been beaten up by a group of boys from Sacred Heart, the Catholic school, but he hadn't cried enough to make doing it again worth anybody's while. So older boys left him alone. And he knew secret routes home, where a hole in a fence could allow for a quick getaway; he knew about strategy and outsmarting the older, dumber boys. Best of all, he had a secret weapon, and whenever Scotty heard it clunk around in Tom's lunch pail, Scotty felt safe. How great, he thought, to have such power. He believed this had kept them safe, and this is why he made sure to walk home with Tom every day he could.

But, in truth, boys from the third through fifth grades had been assigned to their Little League teams. After school, on most days, these boys rode off to baseball practice. They had lost interest in beating up Scotty.

Tom must have known he had the upper hand in their relationship. "You pussy willow," he liked to say. "Scotty is such a pussy willow."

Scotty smiled at these words.

"You're a dog face, a cat lick," Conway ranted. "You're a Q-tip—you're a fart maker."

Sometimes Scotty fell on his knees he laughed so hard. Or he rolled on his back in the new grass, cackling, his legs kicking at the sky above him.

And for a time things were fine.

Then, on a Friday afternoon at the end of April, Scotty and Tom walked home, their lunch pails swinging in unison. At the top of Ashworth Road, those same fourth grade boys—dressed in their new baseball uniforms—biked past them.

Without thinking, Scotty started to shout, "Hey, pussy willows!" Tom joined in. "You're all fart makers!"

The fourth graders stopped on their bikes and looked back. They couldn't believe what they were hearing: Two little runt second graders shouting at them, calling them names. They turned around and started after them.

Scotty and Tom ran, splitting off from each other immediately, as if by instinct. Tom headed toward the empty lot on Twenty-second Street where a new house was being built and Scotty proceeded straight down the street, disappearing from sight as he rounded the corner—unseen, he dove into a mini-forest of evergreen bushes, and began a desperate crawl.

He knew he was forbidden to be on the yard of the Lattimers. They were an old couple who didn't like children. But emergency situations brought about desperate choices—using his forehead to burrow, Scotty went further, deeper into the middle, evergreen needles pricking him. It smelled like Christmas.

He heard the boys shouting, "He's over here!" Scotty stopped moving. He could see glimpses of their uniforms as they circled on their bikes.

The legs of one of the boys kicked at the bushes, almost

hitting Scotty's rib cage, and he saw the legs of someone else, so he lifted a large branch and made one final push into the center of the bushes, crawling deeper in, where he made an amazing discovery—an opening, a pocket of sorts, where the earth dipped low, where the light brown topsoil was smooth and inviting, where God had carved out an almost natural chair, a recliner of sorts that seemed to be custom-made just for him.

And as the fourth graders kicked futilely at certain openings, Scotty waited in his secret spot until they gave up and rode off to their game.

He knew about waiting. He'd been waiting all year.

After dark he emerged and not until then, because he didn't want anyone to see where he was hiding.

It was important to have a place where no one could find you.

(4)

Scotty found himself in an unfortunate situation. With Tom Conway home sick, he was on his own. For a week the two of them had been outsmarting the fourth graders, but now, not only was Scotty alone, he was out of ideas.

The bell rang and the students left for home. Scotty knew that the fourth graders were gathering outside, and he puttered at his desk and then lingered in the hallway.

Before leaving school to confront the inevitable, he went into the bathroom nearest the principal's office. He splashed cold water on his face. He used the yellow liquid soap to wash his hands and pulled a brown paper towel from the towel dispenser. As he pushed open the hinged door on the trash can, he realized the domed lid could come off. It took effort but he was able to pry it loose. To his surprise, he fit snugly into the trash can. And if he squatted down (the used towels made a kind of cushion), he could bring the lid back into place.

This was a good plan, for about an hour, until Mr. Fry, the night janitor, pushed his cleaning cart into the bathroom. It was then Scotty knew he would be discovered.

Mr. Fry was sweeping the toilet stalls when he saw in the mirror Scotty Ocean standing, his bottom half covered by the trash can. "Surprise," Scotty said, hoping Mr. Fry wouldn't yell at him.

Mr. Fry didn't even seem startled. Without missing a beat, he said, "School's about to close up, young man. You better get on."

The school clock read 4:25 when Scotty emerged from the bathroom. His legs had fallen asleep (they felt all tingly). He walked slowly down the empty hall. Outside no one was around. Even the flags (American and Iowa) had been lowered from the flagpole and folded up for the day. Scotty sat under the kindergarten slide / monkey bars unit for a time just to be sure the boys were gone. It was then that he saw Jodi Jerard standing near the swing set, staring at him.

"Follow me," she ordered, and he did.

He found himself standing with her in back of where third grade would one day be. With his back to the concrete brick wall, he watched as Jodi removed the black band and metal hoop that helped straighten her teeth. "Headgear's a pain," she said.

"Yeah," he said, even though he didn't know. He still had some baby teeth.

After setting the headgear down carefully on her pink backpack, Jodi used her fingers to comb her frizzy hair. Scotty looked up at her. He suddenly understood why the other kids called her "horse face," for Jodi Jerard resembled a horse in all ways. Any mention of it now, though, would destroy the mood and possibly bring him physical harm. Wisely he said nothing. Jodi Jerard was, after all, the tallest fifth grader, stronger than most boys, and most notably, a year earlier as a fourth grader, she had set a school record for the softball throw on Track and Field Day.

They stood facing each other. Since Jodi stood a head taller, Scotty didn't know where to look. If he stared straight ahead, her breasts, which looked like the pitching mounds at the Little League field, would be all he could see. He better not look down; a man should never look down. Looking up, then, he focused for a time on her forehead. He quickly glanced at her long, fleshy nose. Then he watched as she wet her lips. Finally, after looking at every inch of her face, and having nowhere left to go, he looked her in the eye. Man to man, he thought.

With their eyes locked, Scotty's from fear, Jodi finally spoke. "I don't like you, Scotty Ocean. Know that first thing. I'm using you, okay? For practice."

"Okay . . ."

"I want to get good. So close your eyes and just stand there." She then instructed Scotty to open his mouth. Using her tongue, she licked around his lips. "This is the French way."

"It tickles."

"Shut up. Just keep your mouth open." He stretched open more; he even stuck out his tongue. Jodi put her mouth up to his, squeezed his head with her hands, and moved about frantically. Scotty felt little nips and pricks.

When Jodi Jerard slowed her mouth assault, she collapsed on the grass, propped herself up on her elbows, tossed back her hair, and turned to Scotty. You're supposed to smile after kissing, Scotty thought. He grinned as best he could.

Jodi froze for a moment. Around Scotty's mouth, on both the bottom and top lips, were numerous tiny red dots. Scotty had been cut repeatedly from her braces. Blood began to dribble out. It dripped down his chin.

And Scotty thought, This must be the feel of kissing.

Jodi offered her sleeve to stop the bleeding. Scotty preferred to use his own shirt. He untucked it and held it to his lips, long enough, he hoped, for the blood to clot.

"You won't tell anyone, will you?"

Scotty looked at her.

"I'll kick you, Scotty Ocean, if you tell *anybody*. I'll kick you where it counts."

Scotty swore he'd never tell.

At dinner, while his sisters told funny stories to amuse the Judge, Scotty sat with a napkin held close to his face, afraid to chew, convinced his lips would split open.

Before dinner Claire had covered the cuts with a tan/beige makeup. While Claire worked, Maggie proceeded to pummel Scotty with questions about how it happened. Scotty said nothing and looked to Claire for help. She told Maggie to hush. After Maggie got called downstairs to set the table, Scotty breathed out a sigh. Claire smiled. Scotty tried to smile but it hurt so he stopped.

"Ow, huh?" said Claire.

Scotty nodded. He appreciated her not asking questions.

It was during dinner, Maggie later claimed, that she figured it out. For she knew of three other boys, older boys, fifth graders, who wandered the halls of Clover Hills Elementary with scabby lips. And she knew Jodi Jerard had been the cause.

That weekend Joan met her children for a brunch at Baker's Cafeteria in the Sherwood Forest Shopping Center. When she hugged Scotty, she noticed the tiny scabs that framed his lips. "Sweetie," Joan said, squatting down to Scotty's level. "What happened to you?"

Scotty shrugged. It still hurt to smile.

"Let's eat," Maggie said. "I'm starved."

"Now I know you kids have been worried," Joan said. "But don't. I'm back on track."

"We're glad, Mom," Claire said.

While they went through the buffet line, Scotty studied his mother. She wore no handcuffs, no prison clothes, and she had no police escort. She seemed fine.

He excused himself to go use the bathroom, and when he came back, he saw Maggie whispering to Joan. He knew she was telling her everything. He sat down in his seat. Joan turned to him. She reached to touch his lips. "Oh, sweetie," she said.

Scotty said faintly, "What?"

"Honey," Joan said, suppressing a smile, "you've been kissing the wrong people."

(5)

"Baseball season, Ocean," Andrew Crow said, holding a Wiffle ball bat. "Do you know what that means?"

Scotty shrugged.

Andrew Crow swung the yellow plastic bat connecting with the Wiffle ball, which sailed over Scotty's head. He brought the Wiffle ball back to Andrew, who immediately swung again sending the ball flying across the Crows' backyard.

"It's time to run the bases."

Scotty said, "Yes," for Andrew must be right.

"Remember the bases?"

An out-of-breath Scotty returned with the Wiffle ball, his shoulders heaving. He thought he remembered.

Andrew Crow held the yellow bat with his right hand and took the Wiffle ball in his left. "You need girls to play real baseball." Smack, the Wiffle ball bounced behind Scotty, who almost tripped as he ran after it. "Ocean, you know what? I almost wish you were a girl."

An exhausted Scotty, winded and about to fall over, needed two hands to hand it back.

"Thirsty?" said Andrew.

Scotty nodded. He was thirsty.

In the Crow house, Andrew put his mouth up to the kitchen sink water faucet. He gulped and gulped, and Scotty watched how his Adam's apple went up and down with each swallow. Andrew pulled away, sucked in a deep breath, and then drank more. Then he wiped his mouth with his shirt sleeve. He didn't offer Scotty any water. Then he opened the basement door, and before disappearing, said, "Come on."

Descending the carpeted stairs Scotty thought this was how astronauts must feel. Andrew had gone ahead. Because he was second, Scotty decided to be Buzz Aldrin, and he took the last stairs backward, hopping down a step at a time, the balls of his feet touching, then his heels, each step moving closer to the orangeish and goldish and yellow-specked shag carpet of Andrew Crow's basement—and when both feet had finally landed, it felt to Scotty that this was as good as the moon.

Andrew had pulled at the appropriate strings, and the room throbbed with light. Three Chinese lanterns that hung equal distance from each other glowed bright reds, yellows, and greens.

Andrew had so much: his own television set, a hi-fi stereo with individual speakers, even an Audio lite, a speakerlike box that flashed bright color combinations to the beat of music. He had a Ping-Pong table, a bumper pool table with a wall mount for pool cues, and a player piano that you operated with your feet.

Shelves lined the walls with stacks of board games—Clue, Monopoly, Sorry, Stratego, Battleship, Green Ghost. Another closet had Dynamite Shack, Don't Break the Ice, Don't Spill the Beans, Skittle Bowl, Operation, Twister, Chinese checkers, Concentration—every game!

"Except for where my mom does laundry," Andrew said, "the basement is all mine."

The laundry room took up one small corner of the basement. It wasn't carpeted; nor was a room in the opposite corner where, lit by a naked bulb that turned on with a hard tug of a dangling string, Scotty saw three impressive sights.

The first was Andrew's tool chest, everything clean and in order, with man-sized tools hanging on a wall of unpainted Peg-Board. The shape of each tool had been outlined in black.

In the center of the room a rectangular piece of plywood (the size of the Judge's bed) rested on sawhorses. On top of the board, an HO train track had been laid. Scotty saw the steam locomotive train with coal car, boxcars, an auto carrier with six miniature automobiles, the remote-control log-dump car with log receiver, a flatcar with three sections of culvert pipe, and an eight-wheel caboose, painted bright red like a bloody nose. He saw a crossing gate, which was to drop as the train approached, a lighted freight station with miniature workers.

Around the train, a miniature town was in the process of being constructed. A mountain had been carved out of Styrofoam, and a tunnel ran through its center. Houses with telephone poles, hand-painted street signs, trees, bushes, and cars had been put out in careful arrangements.

"We're building our own city," Andrew Crow said. "My dad works on it with me."

Scotty wanted to run home and tell the Judge. He wanted to show his father the city that the Crows were making. "Evidence," he wanted to shout. But the Judge would ask, "Evidence of what?" and Scotty would be stumped. This city seemed like evidence to Scotty, some sort of proof that everybody—the Bradys, the Cartwrights, everybody—had it better than the Oceans. But the Crows were close, next door close; all Scotty needed to do was move one house over and all this would be his.

Andrew didn't turn on the train for Scotty. Instead he moved to the corner of the room and gestured for Scotty to look his way. It was then that Scotty saw Andrew's personal gym. A punching bag was bolted to the wall with an adjustable mount. It was set at Andrew's eye level. He reached out, hit it with his fist, and it bounced back and forth. Scotty would have to stand on a stool to be able to punch it. But there was no stool, and Andrew only seemed interested in his own punching.

"It's a matter of timing," Andrew announced. He hit the

bag with the back of one hand, then the other, creating a steady rhythm of the bag going forward then backward, like the boxers Scotty had seen training on TV. "A matter of timing," he repeated, and Scotty thought that Andrew was probably right, not realizing that having the resources and the teacher might also help, and being the right height.

"My dad wants me to be able to defend myself."

That seemed like a good thing, defending oneself.

In the far corner Scotty saw a most impressive sight. A blue metal weight-lifting bench with a black cushion backrest. A barbell, two dumbbells, and stacks of different-size circular weights.

"One hundred ten pounds worth of weights in all."

Scotty approached slowly.

"The big ones are ten pounds." Scotty looked at the circular weights. "Filled with sand." Embossed on the sides, 10 LBS. had been stamped in the vinyl weights. Scotty traced the numbers with his finger.

"I can do squats, bench press, curls, clean and jerk." Andrew bent down and pulled the barbell up to his pelvis. With a single thrust, he lifted it higher, shifting his wrists so the barbell was shoulder height, just below his chin. Breathing quickly through his nose, he prepared for the final lift. He inched his right foot forward, and as he struggled to get the barbell above his head, he grunted like the weight lifters on *Wide World of Sports*. His face turned more red than pink, and the veins in his neck jutted out, his mouth contorted, as if the muscles in his lips were doing their part to help.

He locked his arms above his head for a second, long enough to make it officially count, and then he let them drop. But the weights didn't bounce the way they did on television.

"There," Andrew said, plopping down in one of his matching bean-bag chairs in the game room. "I lifted your weight."

Then Andrew had Scotty try. And Scotty positioned himself under the bench, and he gripped the barbell, pressed his feet to the ground, and using every ounce of strength, all his muscles past and present, he tried to lift the barbell.

But it wouldn't budge.

The only condition Andrew gave Scotty was the following: "Tell your sisters what you saw, especially the one with boobs."

So at dinner Scotty recounted the experience of Andrew Crow's basement. He couldn't remember all of the toys, so he said, "Every toy."

"Every toy?" the Judge asked. "I find that hard to believe."

"You must be exaggerating, Scotty," Claire said.

"No," he said. "You should see it."

Claire explained that the last place she'd ever be caught would be in Andrew Crow's basement.

"But he's got everything."

Maggie blurted out, "I think Scotty's exaggerating."

"We'll have to believe him, though," Claire said, "because I'm not going down there."

"Scotty," the Judge warned, "if you're always exaggerating, no one will believe you."

(6)

Scotty had a dream that recurred. In it he was being chased (he didn't know who or why), but he knew enough to hide. He ran into a room full of mummies. He wrapped himself up. The people chasing him went around unwrapping each mummy, and in each one they found nothing, only dust. Every mummy was unwrapped except for the one where Scotty hid. The people started to unwrap it; they peeled away the strips of fabric, pulling and pulling until all the cloth was removed— but Scotty was gone. He had vanished. And he didn't know where he went.

This is when Scotty always woke up.

(7)

Once on *Captain Kangaroo,* Mr. Green Jeans explained the difference between a good neighbor and a bad neighbor. Mr. Green Jeans's major point: Good neighbors are courteous and kind.

When Scotty stood on the Crows' front porch, he expected to be greeted more kindly. But Andrew looked disappointed when he saw who stood at the door.

"Oh, it's you."

Scotty reminded himself, Good neighbors are courteous and kind.

Andrew barked, "What do you want?"

Scotty didn't understand how a boy could suddenly be an entirely different person. Only days earlier, he got a tour of the basement. Andrew had been *nice*. Now he didn't even want to talk, and Scotty had to shout to be heard through the glass door.

"What was that?"

Scotty shouted again, "You said you . . . !"

Mrs. Crow walked up behind Andrew and said, "Andrew, invite your little friend inside."

Little, Scotty thought. I'm not little. I'm seven.

Andrew didn't want company. But Scotty knew that when Andrew realized what Scotty had brought him, they'd be best friends.

Andrew reluctantly let him step into the vestibule. The house smelled of freshly fried bacon.

"Don't worry, Mom," Andrew said back. "Scotty won't be staying long." Then in a whisper, "What do you want?"

"You said you wanted to meet girls?"

"Yes," Andrew said, suddenly interested.

"Well, pick a hand."

Andrew said, "Get lost, Scotty."

"Pick a hand."

Andrew wanted no part of it. "Good-bye."

Scotty brought his *Bonanza* lunch pail from behind his back.

Andrew smirked. "I'm not hungry."

Scotty smiled because he had fooled Andrew Crow. He wanted to shout, "There isn't food in my lunch pail!"

"Don't want you boys making a mess," Mrs. Crow said as she passed by on her way up the stairs.

"Okay, Mom!" an exasperated Andrew called after her.

Then he squeezed his face into a pursed expression and said in a high-pitched nagging way, "Don't want you making a mess."

Scotty laughed.

Andrew grabbed the *Bonanza* lunch pail and headed toward the basement stairs, calling back, "You got to take off your shoes." Scotty's socks pulled half way off as he struggled to get out of his shoes. Then he ran after Andrew.

Downstairs, Scotty found Andrew had already opened the *Bonanza* lunch pail. Two Barbies were stuffed inside, along with a Skipper and a Francie.

Scotty couldn't help but smile.

Staring at the mangle of plastic bodies below him, Andrew kept his same blank expression. He reached down, picked up each doll by her hair, and let them dangle from one hand as if they were carrots.

Scotty wanted to protest, "Don't pull their hair," but before he could even speak, Andrew let them drop onto the shag carpet.

"*Real* girls, stupid—I want *real girls*."

Andrew stripped the first Barbie of her metallic blouse. He ran his finger over Barbie's bare chest. "See," Andrew said, "there should be nipples here."

"Oh," Scotty said.

Andrew pulled off Barbie's plastic go-go boots and then yanked off her Leatherette skirt. He pointed to the space between her legs and said, "Real girls have a hole here. Real girls have a patch of hair."

Scotty looked surprised.

"You don't believe me?"

Before Scotty could say he believed, Andrew said, "Your sister has got to have hair there. Your sister with the boobs."

Scotty knew Andrew meant Claire. Scotty at least knew that much.

"Have you seen it?"

"What?"

"Her patch of hair?"

Scotty said, "Yeah."

"Bull," Andrew Crow said. Then he disappeared into the back corner of the basement. Following, Scotty entered the dark room. Andrew moved his arms about searching for the dangling string. Finding it, he pulled hard and the naked bulb snapped on, causing Scotty to squint.

Andrew moved to his tool bench and yanked open a drawer that was full of different-size nails. He pulled out another that held nuts and bolts. "Where is it?" he said to himself, opening and closing other drawers, frantically searching for something.

Scotty knew to keep his distance when Andrew was mad. He wandered over to the train set. He noticed all the new construction the town had undergone in the days since he'd last seen it. The Styrofoam mountain had been painted green; more miniature people had been placed about the train track area; and plastic trees, bushes, and other shrubbery had been planted.

Soon Andrew Crow would have his own little town. He would no longer be God's gift, as Claire called him. He'd be God.

But, at the moment, Andrew was an unhappy God, dumping out drawers, slamming tools on the tool bench.

Scotty moved back into the main basement room to check on Barbie. Lying naked and mangled in the shag carpet, her legs splayed and her arms out of whack, Scotty thought, She must be cold. He was contemplating what to use as a makeshift blanket when Andrew said, "Bingo!"

Scotty turned to see what Andrew had found, expecting it to be unusual, something he'd never seen before, for Andrew always seemed to have some toy or object no other kid had.

But Andrew held out a corkscrew.

Scotty knew about the corkscrew. It was exactly the kind Joan had had at her studio, perfect for opening bottles of wine.

"Wah-lah," Andrew said, pushing past Scotty and heading toward Barbie. He knelt down and bent Barbie's rubber legs like a wishbone.

"Hold her down," Andrew said.

Scotty pressed on Barbie's arms, which stretched above her head. Barbie had real eyelashes and rooted hair, bendable legs. "She was part real," Scotty wanted to say.

Andrew jabbed the tip of the corkscrew between Barbie's legs, leaving a divot. Then he began to slowly turn the corkscrew, twisting up shards of Barbie's pink plastic flesh.

Scotty imagined Barbie shrieking.

Andrew twisted and twisted until he'd dug out a hole. "There," he said. "That's more like it."

Andrew stripped the other Barbie. He drilled an identical hole. Francie and Skipper were punctured, too, even though Skipper was harder to penetrate, for she was smaller and had the twist-and-turn waist.

When he was finished, Andrew stretched out on the carpet and stared at the corkboard ceiling. Andrew was bored with the Barbies—he didn't even bother to dress them. He stood up, stretched, and returned to the back room, saying, "I'm going to pump some iron."

Scotty dressed the dolls and stuffed them back into his lunch pail. Later he would have to find a way to sneak back into Maggie's room and put them back in their proper place.

From the basement as he heard the grunts of Andrew Crow bench-pressing, Scotty sat waiting, hoping Andrew would talk with him. Say something. Say something about anything. Scotty didn't care what.

(8)

"After the year we've had, I've decided it's what we deserve." The Judge had gathered his children around the dining room table. They stared speechless at pictures of the various shapes: rectangular, circular, kidney shaped.

"It's a present for the whole family. . . ."

"A swimming pool?" Scotty said in disbelief.

"Yes," the Judge said.

Claire and Maggie were excited, too. Images of the summer began to form in everyone's mind. Maggie pictured boys and more boys; Claire imagined swimming at night; Scotty dreamt of buying the submarine advertised in the back of DC Comics, a submarine that cost all of $9.95. He ran to his room and studied the ad. A periscope. Two people can fit in it. Amazing. He would live underwater, only surfacing for lunches of peanut butter and jelly sandwiches.

Word spread.

During recess Cindy McCameron, whose family had a pool, asked, "You getting a slide *and* a diving board or just a diving board?"

Scotty shrugged because the specific decisions hadn't yet been made.

"We got both," Cindy reminded Scotty.

"I know," Scotty said. Other kids asked questions. Scotty felt his popularity about to increase. Was he crazy, or were more kids sitting with him at lunch, was he getting chosen earlier when sides were picked for kickball and other team games?

Even Andrew Crow was talking to him again.

"Hey, Ocean, I hear you're getting a pool."

"Yep," Scotty replied to Andrew as they each stood in their respective backyards. Scotty had been standing outside trying to imagine how it would look, the pool, and where all the dug-up grass and dirt would go.

"Do you even know how to swim?" Andrew asked.

"Yeah," Scotty said.

"Your sisters gonna go skinny-dipping?"

"Yeah." Scotty thought, What is skinny-dipping?

"You gonna let me go swimming?"

Scotty answered the phone.

"Hey, little love."

"Hi, Mom."

"What are you doing?"

"Picking out a pool."

"You're what?"

"Picking out a pool. Dad's buying us a pool."

"Really."

"Yep. With a diving board, everything. Big tractor's gonna dig a hole in our backyard. Go swimming whenever we want. Building it for summer."

Joan paused to regroup. She realized what the Judge was doing, but she continued with the reason for her call anyway. "Your dad and I had a talk. Did he tell you?"

"No."

"I was thinking you could come to Iowa City with me for the summer. My apartment is small, but it's roomy enough for two."

"The summer?"

"Yes. Your dad said that it would be up to you."

Scotty paused. "I don't know."

"You think about it. We could have fun."

"Mom, the pool could be lots of shapes. There are so many shapes."

"You think about it."

Nothing was said as Scotty switched the receiver to his other ear.

"I changed ears."

"What was that?"

"Nothing."

"Oh."

"Mom?"

"Yeah?"

"You wanna talk to somebody else?"

(9)

As Scotty Ocean and Tom Conway walked home, the sky above them was dark with rain clouds.

Minutes earlier, just before the bell rang, Mrs. Boyden had presented each student with May baskets—little paper drinking cups with jelly beans and candy corn. It was the first day of May. Scotty hadn't touched any of his candy. He was too busy listening to Tom retell something he'd heard his father, the sergeant, say.

"They would . . . uhm . . . tape it, the grenade . . . on the hands of the gook kids . . . and send them back to their people . . . and when the parents untaped the hands . . . boom . . . blown to bits."

"Ow," said Scotty.

"What do you mean, 'ow'?"

"It would hurt, ow."

"It's the way we're gonna win the war. They are the enemy, dummy. Don't you get it?"

Scotty didn't understand. He imagined hands taped with activated grenades. He wondered, What if you got an itch? In that situation, how does a kid scratch himself?

At the top of the Ashworth Road, Tom heard the yelling first. Scotty was deep in thought. But when he saw Tom sprint ahead, he knew he better do the same. Glancing back, he saw that Bob Fowler and other fourth graders were speeding toward them on their bikes. They ran together for a time, but when Tom Conway headed toward the construction site, Scotty split off. He hid behind the Lallys' air conditioner where he attempted to emulate the stillness of a rabbit, and for a moment he was Mingo, the Indian from the Daniel Boone show. He realized he would be found eventually. So he dropped into the basement window well, even though it was full of dead leaves and cobwebs. A snake could be sleeping under all the muck, he thought. Or a nasty spider. But better a snake or spider than Bob Fowler and his friends. Scotty burrowed under the leaves. He heard the boys' feet on the grass; he heard them calling to each other; he heard them getting closer. So he took off, climbing a chain-link fence, running past the Grodts' plaster birdbath. As nearly as he could tell, no one was following.

Two boys saw Scotty as he ran between the Keith's house and the Hoyts' and they took off after him. But Scotty turned onto his street, crouched by the side of the Lattimers' house, and sprinted for the bushes, crawling deep into them where he found his spot, safe again.

Tom Conway rang the doorbell at the Ocean house while the Oceans ate dinner.

Tom said, "Is Scotty home?"

Maggie answered the door, said, "We're eating, Tom," and went back inside.

Tom waited on the curb for Scotty, who came out as soon as he'd cleaned his plate.

"What?" said Scotty, standing on the front porch.

"Come here."

Scotty crossed his yard to Tom, who stood in the shadows of the sycamore tree.

"It's gone," Tom said.

"What?"

"It fell out of my lunch box when they were chasing me."

The following day after school, they retraced Tom's steps. They looked all over for the grenade. At the construction site, Tom sighed. "My dad'll kill me. My dad'll kill me."

It seemed to Scotty that Tom had shrunk overnight—he'd been deflated.

They were both so busy with their search, neither saw that

Bob Fowler and the other fourth graders had appeared and were straddling their bikes, waiting to be noticed.

Scotty saw them first. "Tom," he said. Tom turned to look and saw they were surrounded.

Bob Fowler got off his bike and let it crash to the ground. Oh boy, Scotty thought.

The other boys dropped their bikes in a similar manner. Tom Conway started to cry, for there was no escape.

Bob Fowler made a fist and prepared to hit Tom Conway when Andrew Crow came riding up on his bike.

"What's going on?" Andrew asked.

"This is between us and them," Bob Fowler said.

"Maybe. But maybe we can make a deal."

Fowler had the toughest fourth graders with him. He didn't need to negotiate. "No thanks," he said. "Quit your crying," he said in a snap to Tom Conway.

Scotty bit his lip.

"You can have the other kid," Andrew Crow said. "But Scotty Ocean's mine."

Bob Fowler looked at Tom and Scotty; he looked at his friends; he looked at Andrew Crow, who stood a head taller and who rode a Schwinn five-speed with butterfly handlebars and a black-knobbed gearshift.

"It's a deal," Bob Fowler said.

Andrew gestured for Scotty to climb on the back of his bike. Scotty hesitated, then did as Andrew wanted.

At the construction site, the fourth grade boys took turns kicking Tom Conway. Meanwhile, coasting away in the distance, heading toward home, with a sweet spring breeze blowing, Andrew Crow, feeling Scotty's unspoken gratitude, said to the boy he had saved, "Scotty, you owe me."

When Andrew opened the Crows' front door and saw Maggie Ocean standing in her pink overall shorts and her white, crinkly go-go boots, he looked disappointed. But he held open the screen door anyway. Maggie said, "Hi," as she walked past, leaving a whiff of her Love's Lemon Mist perfume in the air. Scotty followed, forcing a smile at Andrew, as if expecting a "Thank you."

Andrew whispered to Scotty, "Where's the other one?"

"She won't come."

In the basement, Scotty could tell Maggie was impressed with Andrew Crow's secret world. And by bringing her over, he reexperienced the excitement of his initial visit. He saw the stacks of board games, the excellent shag carpeting, and Andrew's hi-fi stereo all through her eyes. He wanted to say to her, "See, I told you," but he said nothing and watched her stare, her mouth half open as if stunned, frozen, and he listened as she kept repeating, "Wow."

Andrew seemed bored by his toys, and disappointed that Scotty couldn't coax Claire into coming over. He gave the obligatory tour of the back room, turning on the train so Maggie could see that it worked. She said, "It looks like *Mister Rogers' Neighborhood*." Scotty was pointing out his favorite parts of the miniature town—the illuminated streetlamps, the smoke that poured out of the steam-type locomotive train engine, the tunnel carved through the Styrofoam mountain—when Andrew abruptly turned off the naked bulb above them.

In the carpeted room, he showed his record collection and pulled back the closet doors revealing the stacks of board games.

"He has every game," Scotty said.

"Every *good* game," Andrew clarified.

Maggie said she wanted to play something.

"What?" Andrew said, suppressing a yawn.

"Something, I don't know, anything."

Andrew disappeared into the closet and moved boxes around, searching for a game to play. Then Andrew emerged holding Twister.

"How about this?"

Scotty yelled, "Yes!" He'd only played at Tom Conway's, and the two times he'd been in Andrew Crow's basement, he'd wanted more than anything to play a game, any game. Twister, the game that tied you up in knots—Scotty could sing the Twister song. A million times each Saturday Scotty watched the commercial between cartoons.

I love Twister, Scotty thought.

Before they could play, Andrew insisted Maggie remove her go-go boots. "Stocking feet or bare feet," he said, "I don't care which."

Maggie hesitated.

Andrew explained, "Don't want anybody to get hurt."

Maggie unzipped her boots, which clung tight to her ankles. They were eggshell-white and Maggie had been wearing them nonstop since she got them in February.

Andrew was busy removing his penny loafers, so he didn't see the first glimpse of Maggie's ankles, the light pink of the bottoms of her feet.

But Scotty did. He watched as she stretched and pointed her feet, then wiggled her toes.

When Scotty sat down to yank at his shoelaces, Andrew

moved toward him, towering over him. He handed Scotty the Twister spinner board. "Later we'll trade off, but for now, Scotty, you do the spinning."

"Left foot blue," Scotty called out. "Right hand red."

The amazing thing was that Andrew and Maggie were doing what Scotty said. He began to spin faster. He barked out directions.

"Left foot green. Left hand blue."

In his periphery he could see them moving, hear them giggling; This was fun!

"Get off me," Maggie snapped.

Andrew rolled off Maggie but didn't apologize.

"Say you're sorry," she snapped.

"But I'm not."

"Oh."

"Don't you get it?"

Twister, the game of knots. Scotty got it.

"I get it," Scotty shouted.

"Not you, stupid," Andrew Crow said. Then he spoke to Maggie: "Let's do it again." He snapped his fingers and Scotty resumed his spinning.

Andrew stretched over her, around her, his legs wrapped, intertwined, with hers. "Pretzels," Scotty wanted to yell. But Andrew kept glaring over at Scotty, as if to say "Keep spinning!"

"Right hand red. Left foot green. Right foot green."

The black needle circled the spinner board. One time the needle was between colors, so Scotty spun again. The black plastic needle going round and round. He called out feet and hands and which color, talking as fast as he could, until he saw Andrew Crow standing before him, his shirt untucked.

"Stop, Scotty," Andrew said.

And Scotty stopped.

"We're thirsty," Andrew said, pronouncing each word with immense care, the same way Mrs. Boyden said words during the weekly spelling test. Andrew repeated, "Thirsty."

Scotty knew where to find Kool-Aid in a pitcher and paper cups that could be pulled out of a dispenser. Andrew whispered, "Take your time," to Scotty as he headed toward the basement stairs.

Turning back, Scotty saw Maggie lying back on the plastic Twister sheet, her body surrounded by bright colored circles. The barrette in her hair had fallen out; her cheeks were flushed, her mouth open. She was panting, which reminded Scotty of the Conways' collie, her tongue hanging down, slobber.

Everyone was happy.

Upstairs, Scotty found the Dixie Riddle cups and the pitcher of Kool-Aid.

Downstairs, "In-A-Gadda-Da-Vida" played on Andrew's stereo. Andrew knew the drum solo and had developed a pantomime imitation, which he'd hoped would qualify for Bill Riley's Talent Sprouts. Andrew could swing wildly at the air with such precision that one would think that he was the actual drummer for Iron Butterfly.

Scotty hurried to put away the pitcher of Kool-Aid; then he pulled at the basement door only to find that it had been locked. He pounded on the door, but the drum solo on the record drowned out any noise he made. So Scotty sat with his back to the basement door, waiting for the music to stop.

Maggie emerged much later. She wouldn't look at Scotty. She went home.

Andrew Crow followed after and said, "No one made her do anything."

Scotty didn't understand. He handed Andrew a cup full of warm cherry Kool-Aid.

Then Andrew brought his pointer finger up to his nose and sniffed around it. He said, "I'm never washing this finger again."

At dinner Scotty studied Maggie to see if she was upset. When she said what she was thankful for, she wasn't specific, other than to say she was glad she was alive. Then she smiled slightly. She appeared normal. The same.

The following day she returned to Andrew Crow's basement, and Scotty wasn't allowed inside. As he paced in his backyard, Scotty decided Claire had been right—Andrew Crow was trouble. He had destroyed the Barbies; what was he doing now to his sister?

It was Scotty's fault.

That night at dinner, the Judge was furious at having burnt the pork chops. Maggie's job had been to remind the Judge to take them out of the oven, but she forgot. She'd been, Scotty decided, probably daydreaming about Andrew Crow. Claire argued that Maggie was only human. But the Judge shouted back, "I told you to remind me!"

As they ate, the Judge continued to yell.

After dinner Scotty walked over to where the new house was being built. Even being several houses away, Scotty could still hear the Judge slamming kitchen cabinets and shouting. It would soon be dark and he had only until the streetlights came on. Then he would have to go home, something he didn't want to do.

The construction on the exterior of the house was almost complete. Soon they'd install windows and doors, lay down fresh sod, and new neighbors would be moving in.

Scotty walked around inside on the plywood floors. He liked seeing the support beams and the frame. The smell, too, of sawdust. Nice. He picked up an unused nail near the front-door area and tried to think up a use for it. As he imagined driving it through the palm of his hand, the streetlights came on.

Scotty knew he'd better head right home. He started to walk; his shoelaces were flapping on both shoes, so he knelt down near a rock pile and tried tying them. But he couldn't so he tucked the laces in his shoe. It was then he saw an odd-looking rock, surrounded by a patch of dead weeds. He moved closer only to discover it was Tom Conway's grenade.

"Scotty!" the Judge shouted impatiently. "Get home now!"

He touched it with his finger.

He looked around to see if anyone was watching.

"Scoootteeee!"

He stuffed it into his pocket.

Then he walked home.

WHAT WAS LEARNED

(1)

After a lengthy discussion and on their third vote, the Judge and his children finally reached a decision: kidney shaped. Maggie had lobbied for a figure eight design, but Scotty wanted none of it. Claire negotiated the compromise. The pool would be seventeen by thirty-three feet, mid-sized, but outfitted with every perk: a diving board, a seven-foot blue fiberglass slide, underwater lights, and a small, cabinlike structure that would house the filter and pump and have storage room for water toys and cleaning materials. Their chain-link fence would be replaced with a six-foot wooden-slatted fence giving them privacy.

The Judge explained that it would take six to eight weeks to build. "If we're lucky, it'll be ready by the Fourth of July."

Claire asked how they could be of help.

The Judge advised they stay out of the workers' way. "Especially on days when they're digging or pouring the cement."

Scotty said that he knew a quick way to dig the hole.

Maggie said, "These men don't need your help. They're experts."

And before another argument could break out, the Judge interrupted. "And do you know why we're getting this pool?"

No one answered, for they weren't sure.

The Judge said, "Because you kids deserve it."

(2)

On the morning of the last day of school, Scotty and his classmates cleaned out their desks. While the others threw away most of their contents (and then ran outside for an extended recess), it took Scotty until lunchtime to fill the grocery sack he'd brought from home. He carefully considered each item: his old papers, drawings, colored pencils, a used Big Chief notebook full of scribbles, a box of mostly broken crayons, his green-handled scissors. He decided to save everything.

In the afternoon, while the third, fourth, and fifth graders attended Track and Field Day out on the playground, Mrs. Boyden had an annual awards ceremony for her students. Each year she made sure every one of them was honored for something: "Most Sincere," "Best Listener," "Most Improved Reader."

Scotty waited patiently for his award. He'd been surprisingly well behaved the last several weeks. Mrs. Boyden did not know the reason, nor could Scotty have explained it, but it was a combination of things: a sadness about his mother, elation at the spring weather and the construction of the swimming pool, and, perhaps most of all, the confidence of having his own grenade, which sat, hidden at home, in his sock drawer.

When Carole Staley won "Best Girl Artist," Scotty knew he would be next.

As she handed him his "Best Boy Artist" certificate, Mrs. Boyden tried to remember an anecdote she could retell that would send him off into the summer happy and hopeful. All she could think of was his naked portrait, however; so she said nothing other than a remark about how she'd enjoyed teaching him as much as his sisters.

Scotty carefully folded his certificate and slid it into his back pocket.

In the final hour of second grade, Mrs. Boyden rushed to review what she had taught them. "So what else? What else did you learn?"

She pulled down the world map and pointed to places. They called out, "France" and "the Arctic Ocean." She reminded them of all they had done. "And remember we learned how to tell time? How to read, how to add and subtract, remember?" She concluded that they had covered a great deal, that all her students were smarter than they were when the year started. "I can only imagine," she said, minutes before the final school bell of the year rang, "what a world this will be if you keep learning at the rate you've been learning. Don't you agree?"

Scotty joined the others in saying, "Yes, Mrs. Boyden."

"Next year you have multiplication and writing cursive. You have so much to look forward to, don't you?"

"Yes, Mrs. Boyden," the kids said.

"I've been teaching over thirty-five years," Mrs. Boyden announced, "and each year I improve a tiny bit. And thirty-five years of tiny improvements add up."

"Thank you, Mrs. Boyden," David Bumgartner said out loud.

"No need to thank me, David. I'm just passing it on. That's what we're called to do, as teachers, I think."

The last day was always emotional for Mrs. Boyden—particularly the moment when she passed out their teacher assignments for the coming year.

Carole Staley, Dan Burkhett, Tom Conway, Jimmy Lamson were among the others who would be Scotty's classmates in Mrs. Tompkins's third grade class. Mrs. Tompkins was the most popular teacher at Clover Hills Elementary. Scotty was pleased.

With seconds left, she said her final words misty-eyed, "Good luck, sweet children." Then the bell rang and the children were gone.

(3)

The picnic had been Joan's idea. What better way to celebrate the completion of another year of studies? It would be nice, she thought, to honor her children who, as the Judge liked to say, "get smarter every day."

The plans had been agreed to a week in advance. Joan had discussed the specifics with Claire, who passed the phone to the Judge to make it official. Joan was to do the cooking, a menu of the kids' favorites: She'd bring silverware, napkins, paper plates, the requisite red-checkered tablecloth and wicker picnic basket. She'd bring everything except beverages. A time and place were determined. The Judge would drop the children off and Joan would return them. The Judge asked that they be home by dark. Joan said, "Of course," and then hung up.

On the appointed Saturday, Claire filled a thermos with lemonade, another thermos with black cherry Kool-Aid. Maggie was sent to find Scotty. She stood on the porch and yelled for him. She listened for an answer. She prepared to yell again when she saw the top of Scotty's head inside the Judge's car.

Stupids, Scotty thought, I'm ready.

"This was the park of your mother's childhood," the Judge told them as they drove across town. "It will have special meaning for her."

In Des Moines proper, near Joan's childhood home, Green Valley Park sat at the end of a street of one-story homes. The park had a few rusty swings, a slide, a chin-up bar, a shelter for rainy days, and a small pond, where Joan had learned to ice-skate when she was a girl.

The Judge checked his watch and said, "What time do you have?"

Scotty looked at his watch. "Two minutes after."

"Go ahead, Dad," Claire said. "We'll be fine."

The kids climbed out of the car.

"If you need anything, I'll be at my office."

"Good-bye, Dad."

The Judge forced a smile, shifted gears, and drove off to an afternoon of work. At his office, he moved around stacks of papers and sorted mail. He wasn't to get much done that day. Thoughts of his children with his ex-wife consumed him. He considered returning to Green Valley Park, and leaving his car on a side street. He'd peer around a tree or crouch behind bushes: He'd watch how his children behaved when they were with their mother. He feared what he'd see. The only thing he had on a healthy Joan was his dependability. When she was on her best behavior, there was laughter and games. He knew the children would choose her over him, even with the swimming pool.

At the pond, Maggie pointed out the colored fish. "Look, that one is gold and silver. That one is gold." She claimed to have seen a fish with black-and-white spots. Claire reported all she knew about fish. Ignoring them, Scotty gathered a handful of rocks and tried to skip them. The first one plopped. The second sank with barely a sound.

"You need flatter rocks," Maggie said to Scotty.

Claire nodded. "She's right, Scotty. If you want them to skip, you've got to use the appropriate rock. Flat rocks skip farther than round ones."

The girls had begun to move around the pond. Maggie held a stick, pointing out more fish.

Scotty moved to the edge of the park and stood on the curb. He looked up the street in the direction of where he guessed his mother would be coming.

"Scotty, come here! There's a whole school of fish!"

"No!" Scotty shouted back.

His hands, he realized, were dirty from the rocks. He wiped them on his shorts but they were still dirty. Was anyone looking his way? No. He dropped a ball of spit into his cupped hands. He rubbed the spit all around. This washed most of the dirt away. He dried his hands using his shirt. His fingers felt sticky—but better sticky than dirty.

"Scotty, you're missing something special!"

Scotty didn't hear her. He was staring at a speck of yellow at the top of the hill. Was it her? Could it be a mirage? He watched as the yellow speck came closer. The moan of the broken muffler and orange sparks from the dragging tailpipe did not convince him. Even when he thought he could make out her face through the windshield, he didn't believe.

This must be a mirage.

The car swerved from one side of the street to the other. It must be windy, Scotty thought. But the tree branches above him and the bushes to the side of him did not move. Even his hair, combed in his mother's favorite way, wasn't being blown about. There was no wind.

Joan Ocean didn't see Scotty. She was busy trying to drive straight. When she suddenly hit the brakes, the tires screeched. The girls, who were still at the pond, looked in Scotty's direction and saw their mother's car stop in front of him, only feet away.

"You came outta nowhere," Joan said with a smile. "Outta nowhere!"

He walked around to the side. She kicked open her car door, pulled his head toward her with her hands, said, "Hello, baby," then planted a long kiss on his mouth. Scotty thought, This is how a girlfriend is supposed to kiss me.

He helped Joan carry the picnic basket to the nearest picnic table. Claire and Maggie came walking from the pond. Joan shouted to them, "I made your favorites!" Claire looked to Maggie. They knew immediately. Yes, their mother had been drinking, but at least she was playful and funny. At least, she wasn't *that* drunk.

Everyone helped unpack the picnic basket.

Claire told Joan she had news and for her to guess.

Joan said, "Mother doesn't like to guess."

"But guess what? Guess what?"

Joan took the last cigarette from a pack of Salems.

"I got my uhm . . ."

Joan searched for matches in her purse.

"My (period)"—Claire mouthed the word.

Joan looked at Claire, who smiled. Maggie jumped up and down. Scotty felt instinctively that the women were speaking in code.

"Oh honey, I'm so proud," Joan said, lighting the wrong end of the cigarette. It flamed like a flare. She threw it to the ground. "You got to warn me about that, kids! Help your mother!"

Claire said three "sorry's," and then, after getting a hug from Joan, stepped back and smiled.

"I'm so proud," Joan said. "And Maggie, you're next."

Maggie pretended she didn't care. But in truth, she couldn't wait. If she were alone with Joan, she would confess as much and tell about her first boyfriend, Andrew Crow.

Scotty, too, had a surprise, and it was in his pocket. He would wait his turn.

Joan stood up, her fingers gripping the checkered table-cloth, and recited the litany of foods: potato salad, coleslaw, rolls. "And my specialty," she said, setting down the dish with the fried chicken. "Favorites for my favorites." She lifted the lid in grand fashion. "Who wants what? We have legs, breasts, thighs. Who wants what?"

Joan stabbed a wing with her fork and held it up. The chicken had been partially rolled in flour and partially dipped in breadcrumbs. Egg batter dripped off it.

"Mom," Claire asked, "is it cooked?"

"Of course, honey. You want the wing?"

"I do," said Scotty.

She plunked the wing down on the plate and used her fingers to hold it as she pulled the fork away. "There."

"I mean," Claire said, "did you cook it . . . enough?"

"Of course. Who wants a drumstick?"

"I do," said Scotty.

Claire shook her head at Scotty, mouthing "No."

"More, Mom."

Joan loaded up Scotty's plate. "That's my little love."

Claire poked Maggie, signaling her to stop Scotty.

"Maggie, Claire—what will it be?"

"Mom," Claire said, "it's not cooked enough."

"Yes it is."

"Mom, I think it's raw."

"Eat up," Joan said. "Eat! Come on! It's your favorite! Please eat! Scotty?"

Then Scotty said, "I'll eat it."

"Don't," Claire said.

"Why shouldn't he? It's perfectly good."

Scotty kept saying "I'll eat it" as Claire wrestled the chicken from him. "I'll eat it."

Suddenly Joan stopped and sat down on the picnic bench. Claire hugged her. It was hard to understand Joan when she cried, but she kept saying the word "pool," and how she wished she could give them one.

Claire said, "But we don't need two pools."

Joan kept saying, "I know. I know."

They hugged for a long time. Finally, Maggie took Claire's place. Joan kept going, and there was no hint of stopping.

Claire walked away.

Scotty reached in his pocket and pulled out his "Best Boy

Artist" certificate. After unfolding it, he held it up. At some point, when Joan looked over, he thought, this is what she'd see.

Claire walked to the Roosevelt Shopping Center where she called the Judge from a pay phone. "Dad, it's Claire. You better come get us."

(4)

Everyone got up early the morning construction was to begin. On his way out to sit on the curb, Scotty was stopped by Claire, who made a prediction: "Life-size Tonka trucks." In truth, they didn't know what equipment to expect, but they did know that that day the hole for the pool would be dug, and some kind of tractor or earth mover would be arriving soon.

Sitting on the curb, Scotty was in for a different kind of surprise. An Iowa Realty FOR SALE sign had been stuck in the Crows' front yard. He ran to get Claire, who was still eating her breakfast of cantaloupe and yogurt. She came to the porch and glanced over at the sign. "So what," she said. "It's no big deal." Then she went back inside.

But when Maggie got the news, she locked herself in her room and cried the entire morning.

Andrew Crow came outside when the yellow backhoe arrived on the back of a flatbed truck. He didn't seem upset, telling Scotty, "We move every year. It's no biggie. Anyway, Cedar Rapids is a much better city." He also explained his theories on moving. "I don't believe in saying good-bye. Can't stand to see all the kids crying."

Scotty knew only Maggie was crying, and even she was to

recover quickly. In fact, by the end of that day, both she and Claire were to develop huge crushes on the long-haired, tanned construction worker who operated the backhoe.

"Dreamy" was Claire's word to describe how he pulled the levers that guided the metal bucket that dug up their backyard.

Scotty shouted at the man, "I got a quicker way to dig a hole."

The man nodded and smiled but kept working.

"I can do it faster."

"Shut up, Scotty," his sisters said. "Let the guy do his thing."

Kids from a several-block radius gathered to watch the digging. Tom Conway told Scotty that he should have sold lemonade.

Inside the house the phone rang. Joan was calling. "I'm sorry about the picnic," she told Claire, who passed the phone to Scotty. "It's for you."

"Who is this?"

"Me."

"Hi, Scotty," she said. Then she told him how proud she was of his certificate. Scotty had left it under her windshield wiper.

Scotty had other things on his mind: "Mom, this guy . . . he's digging . . . he's got a machine . . . it's yellow . . . he's scooped up the dirt . . . like 'Mike Mulligan and the Steam Shovel' . . . you should see it!"

"I'm in Iowa City, Scotty."

"I know. Hey, Mom." Scotty whispered the following: "Nobody believes me, but I can dig a quicker hole."

"I believe you, Scotty."

. . .

That night, an enthusiastic discussion took place recounting the day's digging. And during the dinners that followed, everyone offered their assessments of the progress of the pool. The arrival of the stainless steel ladder and the diving board kept them talking late into the night. The day the blue fiberglass slide was unpacked from its box, Maggie suggested they eat outside. They stared at it as they ate. It was better than they had imagined.

On slower days when the electricians worked on wiring or the technicians installed the filtration system and the heavy-duty pump, only Scotty watched. For the neighbor kids these days were not particularly exciting. But for Scotty, who asked numerous questions and who wanted to understand everything, it was heaven.

At night the Judge leaned back, feeling genuine satisfaction, and listened as Scotty described in detail his interpretation of how it all was going.

The Judge had wanted a "state-of-the-art" pool and that meant Gunite. A newly developed material used in constructing concrete pools, Gunite was a cementlike substance mixed with sand that the workers could spray with a hose. An extensive network of metal rods had been laid around the bottom and sides of the hole, becoming "the bones" of the pool, and on which the Gunite would stick.

"The advantage of Gunite," a worker explained to Scotty, "is that it can be molded easily."

Another large crowd of curious neighbors gathered the next

day as the crew did its work. In no time the future pool went from being a big hole to looking smooth and curved.

The Ocean children couldn't help but get more excited. They barely noticed the moving van arrive and take away the Crows' belongings. Andrew and his parents had left quietly the day before. The last thing he said to Scotty was "Our house in Cedar Rapids has a pool, and it's bigger."

Scotty told his sisters what Andrew had said, and Maggie said, defiantly, "Yes, but his pool doesn't have *us!*"

One night before dinner, near the end of the month, Claire told the Judge she didn't see how the workers could have the pool ready by the Fourth of July. "There's still so much left to do."

The Judge sent Scotty to wash his hands, then whispered an explanation to his daughters. He pushed the workers for the fourth knowing that they'd be ready by the twelfth.

Claire understood. Maggie didn't. "What's the twelfth?"

"Scotty's birthday."

"Oh."

"I want it ready for his party."

(5)

All continued to go smoothly until the Judge woke his children the last Sunday morning in June.

"We haven't been to services in weeks. We must go. We have much to be thankful for."

So the Judge took them to church.

. . .

After the service, it didn't take Mrs. Myerly and her boys long to find Scotty. He had spent the coffee hour playing outside on the jungle gym. As he entered the parish hall, Scotty watched a mother and her children approach him. The Myerlys had recently returned from a vacation in Florida. They were tanned and happy. Scotty didn't recognize them at first. Mrs. Myerly was dark brown, her teeth a glaring, brilliant white. The tip of her nose was bright pink and had begun to peel.

"Hello, Scotty," Mrs. Myerly said. She had a boy on either side and baby Elizabeth in her arms. It had been weeks since she'd seemed interested in Scotty. He stared at her. It felt nice to see her again.

"How have you been?"

"Good."

"That's good," she said. "Tim has something he wants to ask you."

Tim clung to her side. He hesitated. "Are you . . . are you getting a pool?"

Scotty didn't want to answer Tim.

"My boys love swimming. Isn't that right?"

Tim said, "Yes"—Jeff stuck out his tongue.

"Jeff," Mrs. Myerly said, "be nice."

"I'm a good swimmer," Tim said.

"He's a very good swimmer," Mrs. Myerly said.

"At the YMCA, we take swimming lessons. Jeff's only a Minnow. But I'm a Flying Fish."

Mrs. Myerly explained the various levels of swimmers at the YMCA. She listed them in order: Minnow, Fish, Flying Fish, Dolphin, and Shark.

She lit a cigarette. Her cheeks sank in as she inhaled, making her look, Scotty thought, like a pretty fish.

Then Tim listed the kinds of dives he could do: "The cannonball, the can opener, which is the same as the jackknife."

"Tell Scotty about the belly flop you did once," Mrs. Myerly said. Before he could say anything, Mrs. Myerly started laughing at the memory of Tim landing hard on his stomach. Tim started laughing because she was laughing. Everyone was laughing.

Mrs. Myerly exhaled, sending her smoke violently up and out.

As Tim started to demonstrate his favorite dive, Scotty felt a mixture of feelings. He was confused. His mind raced. She's pretty. They're happy. It's been a long time since she talked to me. Tim stretched his arms out and spread his legs, making the shape of an X. Mrs. Myerly, her sweet lips leaving lipstick on the cigarette butt, smoking, smiling. Tim saying, "This is my favorite dive. I call it . . ."

Scotty stepped up and kicked.

He kicked his Sunday best Buster Brown hard-toed shoe in between Tim's legs.

Tim fell to the ground.

Mrs. Sheila Myerly dropped her cigarette and crouched fast to attend to her boy. The rest of the room grew blurry. Scotty heard voices, saw fuzzy figures moving on the periphery. Did he just do what he thought he did? He remembered the decision; he remembered his foot rising up through space; he remembered the feeling of impact. He remembered each moment individually—but now he was putting them all together. How could he be described? Culprit was the appropriate word.

Maybe Claire would say it, spell it, say it again.

Culprit.

Scotty stood for a moment. The people in the coffee hour scurried about, whispering, shocked at Scotty's wrath. This was the feel of God. People had now seen the power of Scotty. He crossed his arms. He felt oddly satisfied.

Tim Myerly lay on the floor curled into a fetal position. He pressed his hands between his legs. His face was red. As he screamed, a white ring of spit formed around his lips. Little Elizabeth began her own crying. Someone could be heard to be saying, "Scotty, you should be ashamed of yourself."

Scotty was about to say, "I am not. I am not ashamed!" when he felt a pull on his hair.

"Ow," he went.

He felt a hand grab his belt and lift him up. Floating in the air, his pants pulled tight up into his groin, he said, "Owww," as quietly as he could. One hand came down on his rear end as the other held him up. Scotty could only see the floor and a pair of men's shoes below him. Shoes he had polished that morning. Shoes of his father.

Whap on his rear end. Whap. Repeated whaps. But they didn't hurt. He found it funny and giggled. The Judge said, "Bad boy. Bad boy!"

Scotty thought, I'm not a boy. I'm seven. Seven is not a boy.

"Apologize." He stood Scotty up. He took Scotty's face in his large hands and made him look at Tim Myerly sobbing in his mother's arms. "You want your old man to kick *you* there? Is that what you want?"

The Judge took Scotty by the hair with one hand and smacked Scotty on the rear end so hard it looked as if Scotty might snap in two. Some hair came out in the Judge's hand.

Scotty apologized but the conditions were not ideal. He

hung his head as he spoke. He could barely be heard, his voice
signaling that any moment he would burst into tears.

It was not the spanking, or his father's rage, or the humili-
ation in front of so many people that finally broke Scotty open.
It wasn't that Mrs. Sheila Myerly would forever hate him.
Scotty wept as the sting of slaps set in because he knew he got
what he deserved.

The family returned home from church, and Scotty was sent
immediately to his room with orders to clean it. He spent the
afternoon putting away his clothes, clearing off his dresser, and
arranging his toys in his closet.

Downstairs it was strangely quiet. The phone rang once.

He could hear the Judge talking, but Scotty couldn't make
out the words. When he'd cleaned as best he could, he climbed
in bed and pulled the covers over him.

Later, when the Judge pushed open the door, he found Scotty
still under the covers. He pulled off the sheets, raised Scotty
up, and shook him.

"That was the dumbest thing I think you've ever done."

Claire and Maggie could hear all the way down in the
living room.

"So stupid I can't even begin to tell you. The boy isn't
hurt. You are lucky! Do you realize that?"

"Yes," Scotty said.

"Clean up this goddamned room. Every bit of it."

"I did."

The Judge opened the closet door and emptied a box of
toys. He dumped out the sack of Scotty's school supplies.

"Clean it again. And while you do, ask yourself, 'Aren't I lucky?' And your sisters—get up here, girls."

Claire and Maggie hurried up the stairs.

Scotty began to clean the room.

"Faster."

Claire and Maggie stood in the hallway.

"Girls, what am I to do? What more can I do? Your brother, help me . . ."

Claire said, "Dad, please, enough."

The Judge appeared to calm down. He spoke firmly. "You are grounded, young man. You are to stay here. On this property. You are to stay here until I say so."

The Judge pulled out Scotty's top dresser drawer, dumping his socks and underwear all over the room. The grenade fell out, and Scotty watched to see if it was going to explode. The Judge emptied a second drawer on top before he or the girls saw it. The Judge began to shout again. The girls cried for Scotty, begging the Judge to stop, to please calm down.

But he didn't stop. Even Tom Conway could hear him—up and down the street, every neighbor, too, if they closed their eyes and listened, could hear him—Judge Walter Ocean screaming, screaming until his voice gave out. "Is this how you thank your father? Is this how you thank me!"

(6)

The next day as the workers plastered the pool, Scotty stayed inside. His room was spotless. It had never been so clean.

Maggie and Claire called up to Scotty, saying that grounded didn't mean he couldn't come out to the backyard.

That night, after he finished cleaning his plate, he returned straight to his room.

Later, Maggie came and knocked on Scotty's door. He could hear the theme music for *Hawaii Five-O* downstairs. "Dad wants you," she said.

The Judge tried to make pleasant conversation over the nightly bowl of popcorn. Claire and Maggie tried to make jokes. These were their attempts to lighten what had been a tense last two days.

Scotty sat quietly.

Finally, the Judge realized what to discuss. This topic would turn the night around and get Scotty back on track.

Answering back in faint voice, Scotty asked, "What party?"

"*Your* party."

Scotty said nothing, for he didn't understand.

"Your *birthday* party."

"What birthday?"

The Judge forced a smile. "You're turning eight, remember?"

Scotty seemed confused.

The Judge said they had better get planning. "It's coming up; it'll be here before you know it."

Claire said she hoped he'd invite many people. "Since it's the official opening of the pool and all."

The Judge said, "Scotty can invite anybody he wants."

Maggie said she wished her birthday party could have been a pool party. "But I was born in January," she moaned.

Claire wondered aloud if a hand-delivered invitation to Tim Myerly wouldn't be just the thing.

The Judge thought it would be better to mail it and enclose a personal note.

As the Judge, Claire, and Maggie tossed around their ideas, Scotty made an announcement, "I don't want to be eight."

"Tough luck," Maggie said.

Scotty said it again. "I don't want to be eight."

The Judge said, "We all get older, Scotty. There's nothing you or I can do about it."

"Except," Claire added, "have the best party ever."

The homemade invitations had a blue piece of paper shaped like a kidney glued to the front. Claire drew on a stick figure of a boy in a swimsuit, telling Scotty, "That's you." Inside, she and Maggie wrote the vital information with Magic Markers. The Judge had told them that a nice party for Scotty would make all the difference. "Help put the last year behind us," he said.

The girls addressed and stamped the invitations, and the following morning the Judge mailed them.

The workers put up floodlights and worked late each night on the final touches. Ceramic tiles were put in, the diving board mount secured. Soon they would paint.

The phone began to ring with enthusiastic confirmations. "Everyone will be coming," the Judge predicted, "because everyone likes you, Scotty."

Maggie said, "Everyone wants to get in the pool."

Claire said, "And because they like you."

Mrs. Myerly called to say she and Mr. Myerly and especially Tim appreciated Scotty's note. Scotty had written "I am sorry" on the back of the invitation. Then he wrote, "*Please* come to my party."

(Claire had told him what to write. When apologizing, she believed, it's always best to be simple.)

Mrs. Myerly called to say she wished Tim could attend, but they would be out of town visiting grandparents. Before hanging up, she said, "Maybe next year."

Scotty watched the filling of the pool from his bedroom window. The Judge was in shorts and the girls in bikini bottoms and T-shirts; they were sitting in new lawn chairs watching the water rise.

Scotty didn't understand their hurry. After the pool was filled, the water still had to be treated, purified, chlorinated. There was much to learn about keeping the water clean.

The Judge never seemed happier. "Come on down," he called up to Scotty. The girls covered their noses with a white cream to keep from burning.

"Come on, Scotty," Claire said.

"Yeah," Maggie added. They both waved.

Scotty stayed in his bedroom.

Joan called to say she was coming to the party. She had purchased a new swimsuit, floral patterned, and bought two for the girls that matched. She asked to speak to Scotty, but Claire said that he wasn't talking much. "He's preoccupied."

"Is he all right?"

"Oh yeah," Claire said, lying. "It's the pool. He thinks about it all the time."

The next day the new fence was finished. It kept the neighbors from watching. Maggie said that it made her feel safe.

Claire and Maggie spent that afternoon planning Scotty's cake. Claire wanted to bake it. They rejected a swimming pool cake. "Too obvious," Claire said. And besides, how would they replicate the kidney shape?

That night, before dinner, the Judge and the girls took their first swim. Scotty stayed inside, lying on his bed. He listened to their splashing.

(7)

On his last night as a seven-year-old, Scotty Ocean came downstairs to find the party preparations were nearly complete. Three garbage bags were full of blown-up balloons. The streamers remained in their packaging. The cake in the refrigerator only needed candles.

Claire was the first to notice Scotty standing in the kitchen doorway. He wanted to try explaining it one more time. "I like being seven," he said quietly. "I like it a whole lot."

"But you haven't been eight," Claire said, "and everyone else here has."

Scotty wondered aloud if maybe there was a way he could stay seven.

His sisters laughed.

The Judge smiled and pulled him close. "I liked being thirty-nine. But I had to turn forty. I had no choice."

Scotty broke away from the Judge. He ran up the stairs to his room, slid open his sock drawer, and grabbed it.

No one downstairs had any reason to suspect.

When Scotty returned to the living room, he held the grenade firmly in his hand.

"I'm seven. I'm . . ."

Rivers came out his eyes. He stood there—powerful, confident, and sad.

"I'm seven . . ."

Claire saw it first. Then the Judge looked up. Maggie was the last to realize what Scotty was holding. Her smile faded. The Judge asked, "Where did you get that?"

"I'm seven. I'm *seven!*"

"Yes, of course, you are."

The Judge started to move toward Scotty.

"No! Don't!"

"Scotty."

"Don't move any closer or . . ."

His hand, sweaty now, squeezed the grenade tighter.

The Judge, his sisters, none of them moved.

Scotty tried to remember the procedure. Pull the pin. That's what you pull. Pull, then toss? He couldn't remember exactly. Throw it? Drop it? He knew he had gotten their attention. They weren't laughing anymore. They were watching now, barely breathing.

"Scotty," the Judge said softly, attempting to appear calm, "please . . ."

Scotty held his available hand up, as if to say "Do not disturb me." Okay, I'll pull this part. He brought his hand down and reached for the metal pin.

It was quick, the Judge's lunge, almost too easy, but he got the grenade from Scotty and held it in the air. Scotty jumped up and down, trying to reach it, but the Judge was too tall.

The Judge studied the grenade as Scotty clawed at him. "Here you go," the Judge said, giving it back. "It's a dummy model—it's used for demonstrating."

Scotty stood frozen.

Maggie giggled nervously and Claire said, "You sure had us fooled." The Judge looked at his boy, patted him on the back, and said, "I'm glad you're still with us."

Scotty lowered his head; his chin almost touched his chest.

For a time, none of the family knew what to do. Eventually it would be another Scotty story to be told to amuse relatives at holiday gatherings, but for now what else should they say?

Scotty asked to be excused.

"Of course," the Judge said.

Scotty turned and slowly climbed the stairs.

Later, the girls checked on him. They reported back to the Judge that Scotty was in bed with the lights out.

"But you think he's okay?" the Judge asked.

"By tomorrow he'll be fine," Claire said.

Upstairs Scotty couldn't sleep. He had imagined it differently. An explosion sending him every which way. Little bits of him scattered all over Iowa. Maybe a clump of hair would land in Davenport—a patch of skin in Ames.

But it was not to be.

Outside, he could hear his sisters and the Judge. They were wrapping the slide with streamers and filling the pool with balloons.

Still, Scotty lay in bed. With his eyes closed, he pressed the grenade against his chest, pressing so hard it nearly squeezed through his ribs and lodged deep inside.

(8)

When Scotty woke up, he looked out his window. It was pitch-black. He dressed in shorts and a T-shirt. He tried tying the laces of his tennis shoes but ended up making knots.

Downstairs, he found the Judge in the kitchen. "You're up early," the Judge said. "I'm making you a treat."

Scotty rubbed his eyes.

"Why don't you go back to bed?"

Scotty nodded that he would.

"I'll get you up when it's ready." The Judge turned his attention to the coffee cake he was attempting, carefully re-reading the recipe on the box of Bisquick. He didn't notice Scotty step outside.

The streetlights glowed. In the east, the sky had begun to turn a rich purple. Scotty walked down the street. The lights were off in the other houses. His neighbors were asleep. When he got to the bush, he dropped to his knees, crawled in, and claimed his spot. He leaned back and thought, This is where I'll live.

.   .   .

When they discovered he was missing, his sisters took turns shouting from the porch, "Scotty!"

He heard them calling.

They'll never find me.

He used his finger in the dirt to make drawings. He printed his name. If he had paint, he decided, he would make cave paintings, if he had paint. And if he had a cave.

The sun rose higher, and it got hotter.

"Scotty! Scotty!" they called.

He could hear it in their voices. They were scared he was gone for good.

When the phone rang at the Ocean house, the Judge answered on the first ring. He was worried. A neighbor from down the street was on the line. She had heard the Ocean girls calling for Scotty. "Just wanted you to know a boy who looks very much like yours is hiding in the bushes across the street." She could see his T-shirt through the branches, and every few minutes, he poked his head out like a gopher, presumably to see what activity was going on up the street.

The Judge thanked the woman.

She wondered if she should send Scotty home.

"No," the Judge said. "Let him be for now."

Scotty had left his watch behind, so he didn't know the time. But he knew the party guests would be arriving soon. He could picture them all in their swimsuits, running from their cars across the hot concrete driveway. All the kids waiting by the water, but no one getting in, because there was no Scotty.

Up the street, his sisters had stopped calling for him. But

he knew he'd hear his name again soon. Eventually, maybe, there would even be a police car.

He could see the sky through the branches. It was full of every kind of cloud. Faint wisps in one corner; a large cluster of popcornlike clouds plugged up another section of sky. The white line of a jet stream cut across directly above him. Around noon, a group of low-hanging, dark clouds raced by, moving at twice the speed of the others. They brought a burst of rain, big, violent drops, and this was always strange: how it could be sunny and raining at the same time.

Joan called from a gas station. She had pulled over during the downpour. She had just arrived in town. She asked Maggie if they needed anything. She was near a store. The Judge took the phone. He said that they had everything they needed, except for one thing.

Water dripped from the branches of the evergreen bush. The floor of dirt got wet, turning the black soil into a kind of mud paste. Scotty didn't mind: It would take a flood to wash him out.

He found a stick and practiced writing it. Two circles. One on top of the other, as if kissing: 8.

And then he heard the sound.

Low at first, the rumble of a muffler, a car moaning, an announcement—growing, the sound. And Scotty began to look about.

The belch of exhaust, the dragging scrape of a tail pipe, splotches of yellow seen through the branches, moving yellow. It was her. She was driving past, heading to where she used to live.

Suddenly the yellow car came to a stop. The engine idled, and Scotty tried to move a branch to get a better view.

He watched her reach over to the passenger side. He heard the car door lock be lifted—then he watched as she pushed on the passenger door. It creaked, swinging until it was open.

"Scotty," she said. It was barely more than a whisper.

How did she know I was here?

"Little love," she called.

He tried to resist, but the pull was strong.

When he emerged from the bush, she saw his face streaked with mud, his clothes drenched.

"Oh, sweetie," Joan said, her hair tied in a scarf, her lips bright red and her dress clean and fresh. She smiled. "You must've got caught in the storm."

Scotty didn't say anything.

"Come on, get in," Joan said sweetly.

Scotty turned and started to walk. He could feel the car moving. Joan drove up alongside him, the passenger door still open. "Don't you want a ride?"

He stopped. Didn't she understand? He was eight. Eight didn't need a ride.

A mother with a car full of boys in bathing suits pulled up behind Joan, wanting to pass. Joan saw that she was blocking the street. She knew to drive on.

"Sweetie, don't take too long. You don't want to miss your party."

She reached across, pulled the door shut, and drove up the street.

Scotty walked. He walked at his own speed, his hair and clothes still wet from the sudden rain. He headed home, even though he didn't need a party. He was eight now, and parties were for children.